THE GREEN INDIAN

PROBLEM

THE GREEN INDIAN PROBLEM

PROBLEM

JADE LEAF WILLETTS

RENARD PRESS

RENARD PRESS LTD

Kemp House
152–160 City Road
London EC1V 2NX
United Kingdom
info@renardpress.com
020 8050 2928

www.renardpress.com

CONTENTS

THE GREEN INDIAN

PROBLEM

For Scarlett

1989

TREES

Mrs R told us to make a family tree. She said a family tree is a type of drawing that is also like a map of our families. My family tree was hard to do, because some of my family are living with the wrong people. I drew a lot of trees. I put myself, my mum and my sister in the first tree. Then I put my dad in the second one. I put everybody else in the other trees.

Because I am in the top group and the teacher thinks I'm clever, she lets me write stories when I have finished my work. I don't think I'm that clever, because I don't understand how spaceships work, and I am still trying to do my Rubik's cube. My dad can do it really quickly, but I can only get one side the same colour. Orange. If I am not working on a story, Mrs R sometimes tells me to go and sit with Michael and help him with his work. She says that Michael needs extra help. I know this is true because Michael does not understand that 2 x 2 is 4 or 3 + 4 is 7. Michael has also been writing his name wrong. He has been writing 'Micel'. Then the other day I showed him how to write it. He copied his name out loads of times and now he can do it right.

Michael is my best friend. He lives in the next street to me, and he is allowed to stay out on his bike when I am in bed. I can only stay out late if it's not a school night and if my mum is in the right kind of mood to let me. That's just sometimes.

Michael lives with his mum and dad, his brother, his sister and his dogs. He only drew one tree. There were too many people in it because he drew his whole family – even his aunties and uncles were dangling off the branches. He put the dogs at the bottom of it, too. It looked like the dogs had scared everyone, so they climbed away. When I had finished my trees, I helped him to spell out the names in his family. I know how to spell all the names in mine.

I live with my mum, my little sister Verity and a horrible man called Den. Den is short for Dennis. I didn't put Den in our tree because he does not really belong there. He is so horrible he should have his own tree with no other people in it. I wish he was stuck in a tree and could never climb down. There should be special trees for people like Den.

My dad is called Graham, but everyone calls him Gray or Grayo. My mum is called Linda, and people just call her Linda. I wrote down all my dad's names on the branches of his tree. I put his new family in the tree with him too. My dad lives with a woman called Tina and my two brothers, Aaron and Kai. When Mrs R was teaching us about families, she said that some people can have half brothers and sisters. She said half brothers and sisters only share a mum or a dad, not both. I think it means only having one parent that is the same as each other. It was a bit confusing. Michael kept saying, 'I dunno what she's on about.' If Mrs R is right, that would mean my brothers and sister are halves, but I think that is just stupid, because you can't have half a sister. Sisters are not like fractions.

I wish my dad would live with us, but my mum said sometimes mums and dads can't stay with each other because they do not like to live together in the same house. I think they should check if they like to be around each other before they get married. I think that would save people from getting sad. I am sad because my dad does not live with us, but I am also sad because I am stuck.

Mrs R said if we get stuck we should try to work things out. She told us to do it on paper like we do in maths if we can't work out a sum. Then she gave us a spare workbook each, just for working things out. She said writing things down helps to work out problems. That is why I am writing this out. It's because I am stuck with things. When you are stuck, it is called a problem, or a puzzle, and it can sometimes be called a mystery. My problem is a mystery because something has happened to me that I don't understand, and I can't work out why it has happened. The teachers say if we try but still can't work out the answer to something we should ask somebody, but I don't know who will know the right answer. I want to work out the mystery by myself, but I think I will have to ask some questions to get some clues. That is what I am going to do. I am writing this down in my workbook, so it is going to be my clue book too. I'm going to take it home so I can keep working on the problem. I think it might take a long time to get the right answer, because it is a very mysterious mystery.

INDIANS

When my dad asked me why I told the other kids in my class that I come from an Indian tribe, I didn't answer. I knew exactly why I said it, but I didn't tell him the truth, because even though I am seven and a half and he is 29, I know he doesn't understand because he keeps telling me a different thing is true. Instead of explaining, I decided to just be quiet. It was because I didn't know how to explain and also because I was afraid of crying in front of him.

'You're not a boy,' he said. 'You're not a bloody Indian, either.'

His voice wasn't shouting, but his face was.

I didn't say anything.

'You're my little girl,' he said.

In my brain I could hear screaming. It was saying, 'NO I'M NOT! NO I'M NOT! NO I'M NOT!'

I ignored the inside shouting and just let my dad say it. I didn't cry until he walked me home. I got sadder and sadder when I was watching him walk away down the street. Then he disappeared around the corner, and I cried, because I knew he couldn't see me. I was sad that he was angry about the lie because I always want to please him because he's my dad. I cried because I know I am a disappointment. Disappointed is when you wish something was different or better. It is very hard to spell. I also cried because I want to be happy and I don't want to wear the skirt to school. The skirt is the reason I lied. The skirt is my nemesis. We learnt the word nemesis in class. It's easy to understand, because all you have to do is think about superheroes. Lex Luthor is Superman's nemesis, and Darth Vader is Luke Skywalker's nemesis (even though really he's his dad).

The skirt is the thing I hate most in the whole world. I hate it more than Marmite and fish fingers. I even hate it more than Barbie dolls and *The Sound of Music*. *The Sound of Music* is a film, and it's the most boring one I have ever seen. I would rather not have a telly than watch it. I would rather look at the wall. The skirt means the other kids in my class think I'm a girl. I am not a girl, though. I keep telling them that I'm not a girl, but I don't think they understand, because they just look at me with goldfish-style faces. The teachers don't understand, either. They think I'm a girl too. It's because my mum and dad told them I am, and teachers never think that parents lie or get things wrong. When I tell the teachers I am a boy they give me a row, and say 'Don't be silly' and 'Behave' and 'Stop telling lies'. When I tell the other kids in my class, they just listen or stare. Sometimes they ask me lots of questions too.

'You can't be a boy because you've got long hair,' Gareth said.

I told him that lots of boys have long hair.

'Like who?' he said.

'Like pirates, wrestlers, Indians and Ozzy Osbourne,' I said.

'Who's Ozzy Osbourne?'

I told him that Ozzy Osbourne is a singer, and he has long hair, but he didn't know who I was talking about. I know Ozzy Osbourne because of my dad. I don't think Gareth's dad listens to Ozzy Osbourne, so I tried to think of someone he would know.

'Gazza used to have long hair,' I said.

Then Louise said, 'Well, why do you wear a skirt if you're a boy?'

That was when I made up the Indian lie. I told everyone I come from an Indian tribe. I am sticking to the Indian tribe story, even though it is a risk, and my dad might find out again and tell me off. I have to stick to the Indian story because it explains why I have long hair and why I am not allowed to wear trousers, and I can't tell the truth because I am seven and a half and I don't even know what the truth is – that is why I am trying to work it out, because it is a mystery. I don't even know why they make me do it. All I know is I am a boy, but everyone keeps telling me I'm not.

I don't think my mum cares that much about girl things. She doesn't keep on about it as much as *some* people, anyway. She does make me have some girl things, but she lets me have the most normal things and gives me a break from the skirt on the weekends. I love my mum and I want to please her, but I do less to please her than the others. I think it is because I am with my mum most of the time, and I find it hard to keep up pretending that everything is OK when I am at home. You can't pretend at home, it's too hard.

My mum always looks sad, but not as sad as some other people, like the poor Africans on the telly. When she smiles she looks very nice. Sometimes I think my mum is sad because of me. I know that she was sad when Mrs R told her about the Indian lie, and I know she was sad when she realised I was sad about the skirt, but sometimes I have seen her get quite happy. She is happy when her sister, my auntie Carol, comes to visit from London. They go crazy when they see each other. They do the same laugh, and anybody who is with them can't help laughing because it is very funny to hear two women doing a crazy hyena laugh at the exact same time.

GREEN

Green is my favourite colour. When I had to choose a workbook, I chose green. There weren't many colours, so it was easy. You could pick either green or red. I like green because it is the colour of grass. There's lots of grass where I live, because there are a lot of mountains. I also like green because I am Green. That is what I want my name to be, even though it isn't really. I wish everybody would call me it, but they won't, especially the grown-ups. My friends call me Green because friends don't care about real names. I like to be called Green for lots of reasons. It feels comfy when people say it, and it feels like it's the name I was supposed to have. It matches up with me. Green is what my real name means, but I don't like to be called my real name because it is a name for girls, and it makes me sad and embarrassed. Embarrassed is when you're sad and want to hide about something. Mrs R taught us that. I am embarrassed when people call me these words:

Her
She
Girl
My real name: JADE WATERS.

My friends didn't always call me Green. When I was smaller, I had to be called my real name all the time. I started getting called Green when we played the game Boy, Girl, Fruit, Colour in the yard. Louise put my real name in the girl list, and I crossed it out and changed it. I put it in the colour list instead. I did it because jade is a type of green, so it wasn't even a lie. My mum said different types of the same colour are called shades. So I am a shade of green.

After the game everyone called me Green, and it made me feel better, and now I am sticking to it, and when I grow up, I will change my name to Green for ever. I'm going to keep my surname, though. I'm going to be Green Waters, because that is who I really am. I have written GREEN inside this workbook. I have written my address, too, in case I lose it – then maybe someone will post it back to me. They might even read it and have ideas about my mystery. They might even work it out and tell me the answer.

SHERLOCK HOLMES

Today we are going to see my nan and grandad. We have to go on three buses, and it takes a long time to get there. My mum is going home after visiting, but I am staying for two nights. I'm quite lucky because I've got two nans. Nan A and Nan B. Nan A is my mum's mum, and Nan B is my dad's mum. Nan A has got brown, curly hair and Grandad has got silver hair that goes straight back. My grandad wears glasses for reading – so does Nan, but she doesn't read many books, only the Bible, so she doesn't wear hers much.

My grandad is one of my favourite people. I don't like to put people in order, because I feel sad if I put some people far down on the list, but secretly my grandad is my second favourite person. My mum and dad both come first, because I love them exactly the same amount.

To get to my nan and grandad's house, you have to walk over a bridge that goes over a little river. Their house is up three sets of stairs. Their type of house is called a flat. I don't know why they call it that, because it is not flat. It is actually very tall, and from the outside it looks a bit like a skyscraper, but it doesn't have as many windows. I've seen skyscrapers on telly, but not in real life.

They live in number 12. Their flat is really big, and there are four bedrooms. My grandad keeps all his videos and books in one of the rooms. He likes to watch the telly a lot, and he tapes all the things he likes. He puts little stickers on the tapes with numbers, and he writes about them in notebooks that my nan gets him from Hyper Value when she goes into town. He has to do it so he knows where all his films are.

Grandad does not care whether I wear a skirt or a dress or trousers. He says it is 'not important'. Nan thinks it is, though. Sometimes my nan thinks I am being naughty, and she tells my mum to make me do more girl things. I think it is because she is old, not because she is nasty. I still like to stay with her a lot, though.

Inside Nan and Grandad's flat most things are brown and orange. The chairs are brown, and the carpet is brown with an orange pattern. Nothing ever feels bad at their flat, even when Grandad plays his opera music or watches the boring news. I think it feels nice and fuzzy inside because the people who live there are properly happy.

I know what mysteries are because of my grandad. I always watch films with him, and some of the films we watch are mysteries. Lots of films have mysteries in them, like in James Bond and Indiana Jones films. At the end of a mystery somebody finds out what has been going on – that has to happen, because it would be boring if you didn't find out something at the end.

When my nan went to work in the pub in the nighttime, I stayed in with Grandad. Grandad doesn't go to work any more, because he got fed up of being in the army. Now he just watches telly. We watched a film about Sherlock Holmes (it was a mystery). My nan always tells Grandad not to let me watch films for old people, but my grandad doesn't care about things like how old people are, or whether they are boys or girls. He doesn't care about stupid things because he is extra clever. He lets me watch his films, and he lets me stay up until my nan comes home, even if it's past midnight.

Sherlock Holmes is a very clever man who finds out about unusual things. He does detecting to find out clues so he can work out the answers to mysteries. I wish I could ask Sherlock Holmes to work out what is wrong with me, but I can't, because he is a fictional character. My grandad said that means he is not real – he is somebody who is made up. If Sherlock Holmes was real, I would write him a letter and ask him to help me solve my mystery. If the Ghostbusters were real, I would write to them and ask them, too. I bet Egon would be able to work it out. The Ghostbusters might be able to help, because they are scientists, and scientists are good at finding out about strange things that have happened. Scientists are like special detectives that keep all their clues in a lab and use science to get answers. I think I would like to be a scientist when I grow up, but I also want to be a footballer. I don't know if you can be both at the same time. I will try to find out.

EARTH

In school, we are doing a project about countries. We had to learn about the different types of places where people live. The main places people live are in a city or in the countryside, because there aren't many other places left. Then we had to draw pictures of where we live. Michael likes drawing more than writing. I like both. I drew Earth, and then I drew my house and put arrows to show which part of the Earth I live on. Mrs R said it was a good drawing, but she wanted me to draw *exactly* where I live. She gets on my nerves sometimes, because she didn't say that before I started my work. Sometimes teachers are quite stupid. I put the Earth drawing in my tray and started again. I drew a bird's-eye picture of my house, my street and my village. A bird's-eye picture is a view from the sky. I put everything on there – the park, the river, the field and the black bog. I labelled it, too. Then we had to make a list of everything that is good and bad about living in Wales. This is my list:

GOOD THINGS ABOUT LIVING IN WALES:

- There are lots of mountains, fields and trees. It means there are good places to play and climb.
- There is a lot of green.
- It is quite quiet.
- You can get to the seaside quickly.

- Ian Rush.
- Dean Saunders.
- Welsh cakes.
- Castles.
- Most countries have stripes or squares on their flags, but we've got a big red dragon on ours.

I always hear people saying there's 'fuck all' in Wales, but I think it's full of brilliant things. Everything I love is here.

BAD THINGS ABOUT LIVING IN WALES:

- It rains nearly every day, and sometimes when it starts to rain, it feels like it will never stop. When it rains all the time, it's a bit easier to believe that story from the Bible – the one about Noah building an ark. I don't think Noah was Welsh, but it must have rained like it does in Wales wherever he lived.
- In school, you have to say and sing things twice, especially in assembly. You have to say things once in English and once in Welsh. It takes ages to do anything.
- You have to dress up in stupid clothes on St David's Day.
- Sometimes, on the telly, they put cartoons on in Welsh instead of English. It is quite rubbish, because cartoons don't sound right with all the strange Welsh sounds and words.
- Nobody plays baseball. I like the look of baseball when I see it in films. It looks like a fun game, and I think I would be good at it. I wish we played it here.

HATE

My mum said I am not allowed to say I hate anyone because hate is a bad word, but I do hate someone. I hate Dennis. He is so horrible, and he makes everything feel black. Sometimes I am having a nice day, and he just starts being nasty for no reason. He is horrible to me and my mum, but when people come to the house (like his mum and dad) he acts normal and nice. I wish I didn't have to live with him. I wish my mum and dad still lived together, because they are both lovely. I miss my dad, even though I see him on Saturdays. My dad is not nasty like Dennis. You can tell by looking at his eyes that he is nice. I think my mum should have stayed with him, because she ended up with somebody worse.

She didn't go out with Dennis straight away when my dad left. She used to have a different boyfriend when we lived in a flat. I can't remember much about him because I only saw him a few times, but the last time I saw him, he was trying to cut my mum's head off with a big knife. She was stuck against the wall like a painting. She told me to go back into my bedroom, but I didn't listen. Then the man who lived in the next flat burst in and rescued her. He threw the bad man out. The rescuer had long ginger hair, big muscles and a motorbike. I liked him, but I did not like the man with the knife, and I do not like Dennis.

When I asked my mum why she didn't like to live with my dad, she said I am not allowed to know until I am older. Then she said that they just didn't get on. Sometimes, if I think about it, it makes me cry. It also makes me confused, because I love my brothers, and I even like Tina. I just hate Dennis.

NASTY THINGS DENNIS DOES:

- Stares at you for ages (for no reason) with his evil, dead shark eyes.
- Shouts.
- Won't let me stay up past 8 o'clock when he is home.
- Throws things/breaks things.
- Scares my mum.
- Tells my mum not to let me do normal things like play football and play with figures.

ROW

Sometimes I row with my mum, and it makes me very sad. I never row with my dad, but I think that is just because I don't see him as much as my mum, and I am always excited when I see him, so I am always good. This time we rowed because I wanted Nike trainers, and I wasn't allowed to have them. Instead, I had to have Nicks. I hate Nicks trainers because they are like reject Nikes that somebody spelt wrong. I wasn't even allowed to have black ones – I had to have stupid white ones. They say Nicks on the sides in tiny pink writing. I think asking for Nikes was naughty, but I'm not sure. My mum kept saying, 'I can't afford them, so stop asking me. I won't tell you again.' She did tell me again, though – she told me all the way down the street.

I didn't mean to row with my mum about trainers, but I never get the trainers I like. I know it is ungrateful because some people haven't got any shoes, but I just really wanted them. Dennis has got loads of nice trainers. The ones I like the most are called Adidas. They are black with red and green stripes. I always try them on when he leaves them on the stairs.

He doesn't deserve to have them. He doesn't even care about looking after his trainers. He deserves the ugliest Nicks in the shop.

Another bad thing is some kids make fun of you for wearing Nicks. Not Michael, though – he never makes fun of anyone, and that is why he is my best friend. Michael doesn't care much about trainers. He doesn't even wear shoes sometimes, and he is allowed to wear anything he likes. He is so lucky because he is allowed to play anywhere he likes, too. My mum would go mad if I went too far. My mum is still mad at me, so I am wearing the stupid Nicks.

FALL

A bad thing happened. I was climbing on the wall that goes around the field behind my street, and I fell off it and landed in a stingy nettle bush. It killed. I was even crying. I had to go home because it hurt so much. I tried rubbing dock leaves on all the stings, but it didn't work. I had millions of bumps all over me. The stings even got me through my clothes. It hurt a lot.

Even though it hurt, it wasn't my worst fall ever. I've had two bad falls that I can remember the pain of. One was when I was up my nan's, and I fell and hit my face on the curb, and the other one was when my dad took me to the park with my friend Emma. She was on the swing, and I tried to run under it before she could swing back down. I couldn't, and she kicked me in the mouth. She had roller skates on, too. It hurts a lot if you get kicked in the face by a roller skate joined to a girl on a swing. After I stopped crying, my dad told me about gravity and motion and forces and lots of other things, which is called physics. Physics is science. It is extra hard to understand. It's OK, though, because I am only seven and a half. It means I have got lots of time to learn. I wish he had explained it before I tried to do it. I don't know why he let me do it if he knew about gravity. I think it was because he was making a fag, so he wasn't taking much notice. Gravity is important because it stops us floating up into the sky, but it also hurts if you try to beat it. It's like picking a fight with someone who is much bigger than you.

When I got out of the stingy bush, I ran home to find my mum. You always want to go home and find your mum when you get hurt, even if she gets on your nerves. It's a silly rule, but it's true.

When my mum was putting cream on the stings, I said, 'I'm sorry for moaning about the girly trainers.'

'It's OK,' she said. 'Forget about it now.' Then she made us strawberry Angel Delight and put it into tiny glass bowls. It's my favourite. She let me have two bowls, one after the other, and I think it meant she was sorry we rowed too.

CONKERS

I stayed at my dad's house on the weekend for two nights because I didn't see him last week. On Friday he picked me up after school, and we went swimming. It wasn't just me and my dad – my brothers were there too. It was brilliant. I love swimming. I didn't say anything to my dad about my swimming costume because he doesn't like it when I say things about boys clothes, so I just wore it and jumped in the pool quickly. Hardly anybody noticed it wasn't the right type of costume; my body was fully underwater most of the time, so you couldn't see anyway.

My dad taught me to swim ages ago. I'm a good swimmer now. I can do four widths without stopping. My dad is a brilliant swimmer. He can even swim underwater.

He can't swim as fast as Johnny Weissmuller (Tarzan), though. Tarzan is the best swimmer ever. Johnny Weissmuller was a swimmer in the Olympics before he decided to be Tarzan. He even won gold medals for swimming. Grandad told me, and he knows everything.

You have to be careful when you're swimming, because you could be swimming along having a nice time and then you could just drown and die. You could also have a swimming accident like crashing into another swimmer or crashing into a wall. There are no walls in the sea, only in pools.

When my dad was little, he was swimming underwater, and a man jumped into the pool and kicked him in the head. It made him bleed a lot, and now he's got a big scar inside his hair. My dad has got a massive scar on his chest, too. It's faded because it happened ages ago, and scars fade like paintings when they get old. It's just like a massive white scribble now. He got that scar because he pulled a teapot on top of himself, and it burnt his skin. He had to stay in hospital for a long time. My dad fell off the roof when he was little as well. I think my dad is very lucky he is alive. I don't think he was very careful about things when he was my age. I think that's why he always tells me to be careful about everything.

I think my dad worries about me a lot because he is always trying to teach me things like what to do if a stranger tries to steal you. Nobody has ever tried to steal me or get me to go in a car with them. I always look over my shoulder to check for strangers when I'm out, though, and I always listen when my dad tells me what to do about things.

My dad says if a stranger tries to talk to you or asks you if you want some sweets or if you want to get in their car, you have to tell them to 'FUCK OFF' and then run. I told him that my mum said I'm not allowed to swear. He said I can if it's at someone who wants to hurt me. My dad also told me and my brothers that if someone tries to grab us and take us, we have to fight them. He said a stranger will be much stronger than us, so there will be no point punching them. Instead, we have to bite them or poke them in the eyes or kick them in the bollocks. Bollocks is just a different word for private parts. My dad has got massive bollocks. I accidentally saw them in the changing rooms. Bollocks is also something people say when they drop a pint of milk on the floor.

On Saturday we went to the park to play football. It was me, Kai, Aaron and my dad. It was a nice cold day, even though the sun was out. We played for ages, and then we collected conkers. The best part was trying to get the conkers out of the trees. We threw branches up, and also the football. There were loads falling out when my dad had his turn. We shared them out and played the game 'conkers'. To win you just have to smash the other person's conker and break it. It was extra fun. I was kind of sad when it was time to go home, because I was having such a nice time. I was also confused, because it is funny when you love someone a lot, but they think you're a girl and you're a boy. It's like they don't really know you properly, even though they see you all the time.

FOOTBALLER

I had to go to bed extra early because it was Sunday. My mum said I had to do it, to be fresh and ready for school the next day, but I couldn't fall asleep. I think it was too early for my brain to be quiet. I was just staring at the ceiling for ages. It wasn't boring, because the plastic glow-in-the-dark stars make the ceiling look like a nice bedtime sky. I was thinking, too, because that's what happens when you are trying to get to sleep but you're not tired. I was still thinking about why I am made to be a girl when I am a boy, and I was thinking about all the things I will do when it is up to me, and nobody can force me to do things any more. The main things I want to do are just normal things. I want to wear trousers and jumpers, and I want to play football, and I think I would like to get married. I would also like to have my own dog. Imagining it made me feel happy enough to fall asleep.

I woke up because I could hear my mum crying. It was very dark, and my eyes were still asleep, but I knew that Den had made her cry because he was shouting. He is the worst man in the world, and I hate him. He makes everything cold and empty and disgusting. I know he is her boyfriend, and he is my sister's dad, but I don't understand why she would pick somebody who is so nasty to her. She used to smile more before he was here. When I grow up, I won't be a nasty man like Den. I'll be a nice man like the men on the telly. I will have a checked shirt and a nice, clean moustache.

Hearing my mum cry is the worst noise in the world. I pulled the blanket over my head because I couldn't stand the noise, and I tried to go back to sleep. I put my hands over my ears, and I thought about football and how it feels when you play football in the night. I was thinking about it because I love the feeling when you're still out and the lamppost lights come on, and the street is dark except for the orange glow, and you can only just see the ball, but you keep playing anyway, and everything feels fuzzy inside you because you're so happy and free.

THE PUB

Today was a good day because I went to work with my nan. My nan (A) works in a pub called The Little Lion. It's called the Lion for short. I don't know why it is called that, because there are no lions where we live, except in the zoo. We went to the zoo on a school trip last year. Everyone loved it, but me and Michael hated it. It was like a giant jail for animals. We saw a lion there. It lived in a tiny cage, and it looked like it had been crying. I think it was just fed up of being stared at and it felt stuck. I didn't like it. I like going to the pub, though.

It's good when I'm at work with Nan, because I am allowed to eat crisps and drink Coke and do what I like (except go into the cellar). I love the smell of it inside the pub. The smell is beer mixed up with the polish that my nan uses to clean the bar. My nan does all different kinds of work. She cleans and serves drinks and makes food that people eat in the restaurant. The restaurant is joined to the pub by a special door. It is also very hard to spell. I had to look in my dictionary to write it.

Nan sometimes works in the night-time, and I am not allowed to go then, but when she works in the day I am allowed to go with her, because hardly anybody is there. Most of the time it is just my nan and some old men who sit in the corner reading newspapers. I don't think they like to be at home very much, because they are always in the pub.

When I was sitting on the stool by the bar, eating salt and vinegar McCoy's crisps, one of the newspaper men came over and asked for a new glass of beer. He had a voice like chocolate, and he was extra clean and tidy. His shirt was tucked into his trousers, which were completely grey, except for a tiny orange label on the pocket which said *F*.

He said, 'Fancy a game of pool, kid?'

I said, 'No thanks.'

I wanted to play, but I was a bit scared, because even though I had seen him before, he was still a stranger. Then he told me his name was Derek, and I decided he probably wasn't going to try and steal me or kill me, because my nan was watching.

'I don't know how to play it,' I said.

'C'mon, it's easy. I'll teach you.'

My nan said it would be OK, and the pool table is not far away from the bar, so I decided to try it. I could still see her, anyway.

Derek told me all the rules, and he was very good at explaining, because he kept saying the same thing over and over again, which made me remember. He showed me how to hold the pool cue properly, and he didn't get annoyed or shout if I didn't understand something, and he didn't mind if I kept asking questions. I wasn't very good at first, but after a couple of games I got better. I didn't scratch the table or pot the white ball. They are the main things that you mustn't do. When I took a shot and missed the ball I aimed for, Derek said, 'Hard lines, kid, hard lines.' I didn't know what hard lines meant, but I think it meant unlucky. When Derek went home, I carried on practising on my own. I like pool. I like the sound the balls make when they hit each other and the sound they make when they go down the pockets and into the special tubes inside the table. I think I will play it again next time I am there. It is my second-best game now.

VIDEOS

We were walking home from school when my mum told me the good news.

'I've got us a video player,' she said.

'Like Grandad's?'

'Yes, so you can watch videos and tape things.'

'How did you get it?' I said.

She laughed and said, 'It fell off the back of a lorry.'

If somebody says that it means 'Don't ask'. It's also a white lie.

I didn't care, though. I was so happy. It was better than Christmas.

Because we've got a video player, it means I can watch *Ghostbusters* every single day. My mum knows how much I love films. That's why she got it. She thinks it is clever that I know what everyone will say before they say it, but she hates it if I copy the accents of the Ghostbusters. I always copy people's accents and voices, and it drives my mum mad. She says it is called mimicking. She hates it most when I do the black and white men's voices from Grandad's films. They're my favourite. They sound extra smart when they speak. My mum goes mad if I do the voices. She says, 'Why are you talking like that? Stop it.' She says she only wants to hear my voice. I wish I had a voice like the men from the films, though. They sound nicer than the people in the real world. Grandad told me all their names and everything about them. He's even got pictures of some of them on the landing. The men who live in the pictures are called James Stewart, Montgomery Clift and James Dean. James Stewart has got the best voice, but James Dean has got the best face. I like him the most. I want to be like him when I grow up.

I don't think it's clever to know all the words from films. I only know the words to *Ghostbusters* because I care, and I have watched it so many times. I can even say the words before the actors. It's just because it's my favourite film. It's my favourite because it is funny and exciting and interesting all at once. My cousin Luke has got all the Ghostbusters figures, and he's got Ecto-1, a proton pack and the ghost trap. When we go to see Auntie Sandra and Luke, me and Luke always play Ghostbusters. We pretend to catch ghosts upstairs, and my mum and my auntie drink coffee and smoke cigarettes downstairs. Luke always wants to be Ray Stantz, and I am always Peter Venkman. I always pretend that Den is trapped in the ghost trap.

Luke has got two rooms. He's so lucky. He's got a normal bedroom and a room next door, which is his playroom. There's no furniture inside it, just loads of toys. You can only see little patches of the carpet. The pattern on it makes you feel like you are looking into a kaleidoscope. My mum had to spell kaleidoscope for me because I couldn't find it in the dictionary. It was even hard for her to get right, and she's nearly 30.

Everyone knows that Luke is a boy, so *he* is allowed to have boys' toys. He's got all the Star Wars figures, loads of cars and a giant garage. I haven't got many good toys, because everyone keeps buying me the wrong type. They keep buying me girls' stuff. The best thing I have got is my bike. It's a red and white BMX. My nan (B) bought it for me last Christmas. I like playing with Luke and his toys, though. He is fun to play games with, even though he sometimes gets in a bad mood if he can't choose the game we play.

Sometimes, if my nan isn't working in the pub at night-time, we are both allowed to stay at her flat. We can't both stay if it's just Grandad, because we make too much noise and 'drive him up the bloody wall'. My grandad is nice, but he likes to hear all the words on the telly, especially if he is watching the news. It's fun to stay at Nan's together, but sometimes we argue because Luke is always allowed to choose the film we get from the video shop. My nan says, because I'm the oldest, I have to let him have his own way. Luke is nice, but he doesn't always listen about taking turns. I don't care, though. We always have fun. It doesn't matter who picks the film.

The video shop is right up the hill from my nan's flat. You have to walk over the bridge to get there. It's next to the off-licence. The off-licence is where you get whisky and wine. I know because it's my dad's best shop. The video shop is mine. Inside the video shop, there is a fire – not a proper fire, a fire that works by gas. The video shop man has got long hair and two sheepdogs. One of them has got different-coloured eyes. One eye is blue, and one is brown. The dogs always sit in front of the fire. The video man says we can stroke them, because they are just old and daft. The video shop man is nice, and he doesn't charge my nan if we take the videos back late. I like him. I would like to work in a video shop when I am older, but I would also like to be a scientist, and a footballer. I can't always decide what I want to do, because there are so many good things to be, but I definitely want to be my real self, which is an M and not an F. Sometimes, when I'm watching a film, I pretend I am the man in it, and then I feel happier because I feel more like myself, a boy. A male and NOT a female.

CARS

We went to the big shop after school. The big shop's real name is the Supermarket. Sometimes my mum buys me a Matchbox car when we go shopping, but most of the time she can't because she is too poor to afford it. If my mum hasn't got enough money to buy me a car, I steal one. I know it's wrong, but I love cars, and they only cost ninety-nine pence. It's less than a quid. I wouldn't steal one from a normal person, but the supermarket man is rich and invisible, so it doesn't feel *that* wrong.

The cars are inside plastic packets, and they have loads of them on little hangers. It takes me ages to choose one, because I love all the colours and all the different makes. The way I steal a car is by holding the one I want for a long time. Next, I check to see if anyone is looking, and then I put it inside my jumper, or sometimes in my trousers, if I am not wearing my uniform.

I love cars, and they are one of the toys I am allowed to have. My favourite car is a Jaguar. I am going to drive one when I am a man. For now, I have got a toy one.

It's a dark green XJS. My mum wants a car, because she hates going on the bus with lots of heavy bags of shopping. She is doing her driving lessons so that one day she can drive. She had to save all her family allowance for ages to afford the lessons. She gave up going out to the pub, too, even though she hardly ever went. Driving lessons cost a lot. My mum really wants to drive a car, though. It is her best plan. I hope she is going to drive us far away from Den.

Michael likes cars too. We play cars in the street if we are not playing football or cowboys and Indians. Michael doesn't care if I am a boy or a girl, he just likes us to play together, and it always makes me happy. Sometimes we climb trees and go and play over in the field behind my house. Last week Michael started crying because he fell in the river and lost one of his shoes. He tried to catch it, but it just drifted away, and then it sank. His socks were black and full of mud. He said his dad would kill him. I don't think anyone has ever been killed for getting mud on their socks or losing one shoe, but Michael was scared to go home. When his dad found out about the lost shoe, he didn't kill him, but he did go mad. He said, 'Get in now, before I give you a pasting.' Michael's mum and dad are nice, but they are quite different to mine. Michael's mum is called his mam and not his mum. It means the same, though. It doesn't matter what you call your mum, she's still one of the most important people in the world. It's the rules.

GHOSTBUSTERS

When I was watching *Ghostbusters* after school, Dennis picked the telly up and threw it through the back door. The back door is in the living room, so he didn't have to chuck it very far. He didn't turn it off first; he just picked it up and threw it all at once. The door smashed, because it was made of glass, then everything was all a blur because of the shouting. I didn't move off the settee for a long time.

It happened when it was the part of the film where Dana Barrett is unpacking her shopping, and eggs start cooking by themselves on the kitchen worktop. Then Dana goes over to the fridge, and the ghost Zuul is inside it.

I don't think Dennis likes *Ghostbusters*. He is always sick of me watching it. I still think that it is stupid to throw the telly out into the garden, though. He could have just asked me to turn it off. I would have listened. My mum was crying again, and I wanted to help her, but she made me go upstairs in case I got glass stuck in my feet. Then my sister started crying, but I don't think she knew what was really going on, because she is only three. She knew it was bad, though – even tiny people can tell when something is *that* wrong.

When Dennis went away, my mum had to ring the council to come and fix the door because it was an emergency. I looked after Verity when she went to the phone box. They came extra quickly. I think it's because we would freeze if they didn't turn up.

It was yesterday's stew for tea. After I had finished my food, I went to check if the video player was broken. I think it is OK, because when Den picked the telly up the wire that joins them together came out, and the video player stayed on the shelf. The green light came on when I pushed the operate button, so I think it just turned itself off.

Verity fell asleep, so my mum carried her up to bed, but I stayed up. Then she put music on her ghetto blaster and did the ironing. The music she put on was Tracy Chapman. Tracy Chapman is a woman, but at first I thought she was a man, because she has got an extra-deep voice. My mum's favourite song is 'Fast Car'. She always rewinds it and plays it over and over again. I think it's because it makes her think of passing her driving test and escaping. I like that song, and I like Tracy Chapman, but I really love the other tape my mum always plays. It is a tape of a woman called Dolly Parton. She sings a brilliant song called 'Jolene'. My mum knows all the words. I don't know what Dolly Parton looks like, because I have never seen a picture of her, but she has got the prettiest voice I have ever heard. When she sings, it sounds like the sun is talking to you. She sounds like sunshine, even when she's singing a sad song. If the sun could talk, I think it would sound exactly like that lady called Dolly Parton. The sun can't talk because it is a ball of fire that heats our planet, so it is warm enough to live on. It is also a giant star. I learnt about it from my book about space.

I stayed up extra late to keep my mum company, and I did some of my colouring book at the same time as listening to the music. I couldn't watch the telly, anyway. If I had a proton pack I would blast Den and get him into a ghost trap, and then he wouldn't be able to ruin everything all the time.

AUNTIE GAIL

When my dad picked me up, we walked to my auntie Gail's house. She lives in the same street as my dad. There were lots of people inside. This is a list of all the people:

Me
My dad
Auntie Gail
Uncle Russell
Jodie (my cousin)
Tina (my dad's girlfriend)
Aaron (my brother)
Kai (my brother)
Nan (B)
Iris (Auntie Gail's funniest friend).

It is quite strange having two families, but it means I'm extra lucky, especially when it's my birthday, and there's money in my cards. The difference between my dad's family and my mum's family is just noise. My dad's family are very loud, and they all talk at the same time. It sounds like a million crows are going nuts because it is nearly their bedtime. Also, it means everybody tries to talk the loudest, just to be the one that gets listened to. They think my mum is extra posh because she talks nice and quietly. They sometimes call her Miss England or Lady Di. I don't know what it means, but I think it means she is a bit like that princess lady called Diana.

Auntie Gail looks unusual. She has got big brown eyes and red hair, which is cut in a shape called a wedge. Uncle Russell has got no hair, which is called bald. I don't see my uncle as much as my auntie because he works shifts in a factory, and he sleeps the wrong way around, in the day instead of the night, like a bat.

I love going to Auntie Gail's. It is always warm, and it's full of laughing people and nice food. I love being there with my dad. I love being with my dad wherever we go, even though he doesn't always understand me properly because of the girl mistake. One of my favourite things about my dad is his smell. I love the smell of his skin. He smells like trees that have been rained on. I love his wonky smile, and his bendy hair, and his kind eyes, which are the colour of conkers. I even love the big scar on his chest, and his tattoos. One of the tattoos is a Welsh dragon. It's all blurry. I don't think it looks like a dragon, though – I think it looks like a giant cat.

My dad's favourite things are alcohol and sports. He loves rugby and football, and he even watches dogs race, which is quite silly. My dad loves all sports except cricket. He said cricket is so boring that the players have to stop and have tea and sandwiches in the middle of the game to stop them falling asleep on the pitch. I quite like the look of cricket, though. Watching sport with his friends makes my dad happy – unless his team loses, then he frowns a lot.

After he had two coffees and three fags, my dad took us to the park to have a kick about. He can kick a ball nearly as high as the clouds. Kai is crap. He always falls over. It's only because he's little. Aaron is good, though. I am getting better at football because I practise every day with Michael.

It was quite cold, so we couldn't play for long, and it was nearly time for the match to start on the telly. On the way home, we went to the shop and bought sweets. I had sherbet lemons and Aaron and Kai had Jelly Tots. Then we played in the living room when my dad watched the football with his friends. His team won, and he drank all his beer and sent his friend Mark to the shop for whisky. It was very smoky in the house, which is one thing I don't like, but everyone was quite happy. When my dad's friends all went home, we watched *Blind Date* on the telly. It's a programme about a girl finding a boyfriend and going on holiday with them. After that, we had Chinese food, and we were allowed to stay up late to watch *Predator*. It was extra good.

LES SEALEY

Today I had my haircut. My mum never lets me get my hair cut short, and on the way to the hairdressers we had a row because I was nagging for a short cut. It is because I am sick of looking like Rapunzel. In the end she said she would think about it, but when grown-ups say they will think about something, it just means they are saying no, but they can't be bothered to talk about it. I was only allowed to have a trim. A trim is just like teasing.

I want my hair cut short because I hate it so much, and it makes me look girly. I even cut a part of it myself before, but it made my mum cry, so I can't do it again, even though I want to cut it all off and put it in the bin. I just have to wait.

When I go to the toilet, I always use water to push my hair back away from my face, then it looks better, apart from the long part at the back. I like my hair pushed back off my face because I hate it when hair touches my eyes and tickles me. I also like the way it looks and feels when it goes backwards. My grandad wears his hair pushed back off his face, but I'm not sure why he wears his hair like that. I think it is because he wants to look like the men in the black and white films he watches. Also, Tarzan has pushed-back hair, and my grandad loves him.

The other man I've seen with hair going backwards is Les Sealey. Les Sealey is one of my favourite footballers.

He is the goalkeeper for Luton Town. I do not support Luton Town, but Les Sealey was the player on the first football card I ever had. Luke gave it to me because he had a doubler. It was before I started collecting them. I've got loads now. My mum gets them from the little shop. I think Les Sealey pushes his hair back so it doesn't get in the way of him seeing the ball. He used to have it flat. I know because I've seen him loads of times on other cards. He used to have very flat hair, and once he even had sideways hair. I think it got in his way, though. Or it might have just got on his nerves. I am going to have my hair like Les Sealey's when I am old enough to choose my own haircut. Les Sealey is the best.

CLUES

CLUES FOR SHERLOCK HOLMES AND
THE GHOSTBUSTERS AND REAL SCIENTISTS:

- All the people I know tell me I am a girl.
- I am a boy inside my brain, but my body is not mine – it belongs to a girl.
- I am not being naughty like my nan and auntie think I am.
- I am just being myself.
- I don't understand what happened to me.
- I am sad because of the mix-up.

WORKINGS OUT/DETECTING:

- My mum and dad wanted a girl, so they prayed for one, but it went wrong, because you get what you are given.
- God was tired or angry when he made me, and he put my brain into the wrong body by mistake.
- I am a reject person, and if I was a toy I would go in the reject bin, like the Raggy Dolls in the cartoon. I am a bit like Back-to-Front, except I am jumbled up in a different way to him. My inside doesn't match my outside.
- I am an accident.
- I am a runt. A runt is a dog that is small or ill, and sometimes runts can have things wrong with them. When animals have babies that are wrong, sometimes they ignore them or kill them or eat them. If I was an animal, I think one of these things would happen to me. If I was a dog, I would die in a basket because my mum would ignore me. I don't think my mum would eat me, because my mum doesn't eat much.

JAGUARS

My mum has passed her driving test. Even though we haven't got a car, she is very happy. She came into the school to tell me when I was in class. I don't think you are supposed to do that, but sometimes my mum doesn't care about things like teachers and being in class and what you

47

are supposed to do. She is not the same as other mums. She doesn't even look like them. Nobody else's mum wears cowboy boots or a leather jacket, and nobody else's mum has got huge curly hair. My mum doesn't sound like anybody else's mum, either. When she speaks, she sounds like the queen. I think it is because she went to school in England and that's where the queen lives. She had to live in England because the army sent Grandad there. My mum's still Welsh, though, she's just got a different accent to me.

Sometimes I am glad that my mum is *my mum* and I haven't got a different one, because I think a different mum might be nastier to me about girl things. I think this because sometimes my auntie and my nan tell my mum to make me into a full girl, but my mum doesn't listen.

When she came into the classroom, she was wearing a black wool jumper with a big snowman on it. It was funny because it is not snowing or Christmastime. I was happy about her passing her test because she was happy. I was also happy about it because I hate going on the bus, and I want to get away from Dennis. I want my mum to drive us, because then we will be able to go anywhere we want. Michael didn't believe it. He said, 'Women can't drive. They're not allowed. Only men can do it.' I told him that my nan B (my dad's mum) drives a red car, but he wouldn't listen. I think it is because he hasn't seen any women drivers and also because he doesn't understand some things (like maths). If I finish my work quickly, I always help Michael with his work, and then he understands it. I think Mrs R should sit with him, though. It is her job, not mine.

Michael is extra nice. He's my favourite person that's not in my family. I don't even care about his black teeth. Sometimes people make fun of him and call him Black Jack, because his teeth look like the sweets, but I don't. He doesn't make fun of me for girl things either. You don't care about each other's wrong parts when you're best friends. You even forget to notice.

My mum was in a lovely mood at home time, and I found out some more good news. She had borrowed a telly from her friend because they have got two and said we could lend one. Nobody has two tellies. They must be rich, or just lucky. I felt lucky because it was such a good day. We were even allowed to have Chinese food instead of normal tea because my mum was too happy to cook. On the way to the Chinese, I asked my mum when she will get a car. I told her to get a Jaguar, because they are the best cars, and I showed her my XJS in case she didn't know what Jaguars look like. I didn't tell her it was stolen, though. My mum doesn't ask where I get all my cars. I don't think she spots the difference between the stolen and bought ones. She laughed when I asked her to get a Jaguar. I think it is just because she is still happy. It was a good night because of the Chinese and the driving test. My mum was still extra happy, and Den hasn't been back since he broke the door. I hope he never comes back, but I know he will. My nan said, 'He's a bad penny, and they always turn up.'

MARGARET THATCHER

When my dad came to pick me up, he had a row with my mum. The row happened because my dad is supposed to give my mum money to help pay for me, but he hardly ever does. I was going to my dad's house, and I wanted to go, but I felt bad for leaving my mum. I felt bad for my dad, too, because he hasn't got a job. A job means you do some work and then you get paid money. When I asked him why he hasn't got one, he said it was Margaret Thatcher's fault. I saw Margaret Thatcher on the telly. She was wearing a blue skirt and jacket, and she was speaking in a strange way. It sounded like she was shouting and whispering at the same time. She is quite scary, but I don't know why it's her fault.

My dad hates Margaret Thatcher. He said it's because she took his job (not the job of Prime Minister, a job in the coal mine). It was a long time ago. He's on the dole now. It means he's allowed a tiny bit of money for nothing. It's so he doesn't starve or die. Dad calls Margaret Thatcher 'Maggie the fucking witch' and other words I mustn't say. He kept moaning about her when we were walking to his house. I said, 'Would you be able to get a new job if Margaret Thatcher died?' He didn't answer. He just laughed. He didn't look very happy, though.

Dad said Maggie hates poor people and football. I don't know why anyone would hate football. I hope she doesn't try to ban it. I wouldn't listen even if she did. Nobody can take football away from you. Even if they took your ball, you could borrow one or join in on somebody else's game. There's always someone playing footy somewhere. Even if you haven't got a pitch, you can play in the street. You can use bins or jumpers for the goal posts. Even if nobody had a ball, you could use a can, or a stone if you had to. Football is free, and nobody can take it away from you, not even Margaret Thatcher.

I think my dad is sad sometimes, even though he laughs a lot. I can tell it when I look into his eyeballs. I think Margaret Thatcher might be sad too, because she never smiles. I think she hates being Prime Minister. I think somebody else should have a turn. I think it should be my grandad, because he is very clever, and he is always fair. He also looks very smart because he used to be in the army. They made him dress smart and polish his boots, and now he can't stop. He doesn't know how to be scruffy. He always combs his hair, and if he is going somewhere special he always wears his navy blazer with the gold buttons and his red striped tie. He even walks smart. He has also got a very kind voice, and I think people would listen to him. I wish I had a voice like him. He always tells me to speak clearly and stop mumbling, but I sometimes forget. You have to have a good voice to be the Prime Minister. You have to have good ideas, too. If I was the Prime Minister, I would make sure everybody had enough food and some-where to live. I would also tell people they could be whatever they want, as long as they didn't want to be a murderer.

When we got to Dad's house, he gave me and my brothers a bar of chocolate each. I had a Mars bar. *Blankety Blank* was on. I don't like *Blankety Blank*; neither does Aaron, so we just played upstairs instead. We got bored of every game though, so we didn't play for long. Stupid *Blankety Blank* was over when we came back down.

My dad was in a much better mood, too. He was burning something brown on his knife and then putting it into his fag (which he made himself by sticking fag papers together in a pattern). When he smoked it, his eyes fell down at the edges, and he was nearly falling asleep, even though it wasn't late. I don't think he should smoke it if it makes him that tired. Grandad doesn't get tired when he smokes. I think it is because he smokes John Player's. I think my dad should swap and smoke them instead.

EASTENDERS

Dennis is back, and he is pretending to be a nice person. It's just an act, though. He can make his voice act, but his eyes catch him out because they always tell the truth. He bought my mum a guitar. He gave it to her as soon as he walked in, even though we had visitors. The visitors were Dennis's friends. I think Grandad would call them 'stupid bloody people' because that is exactly what they are. They laugh at things that aren't funny and talk rubbish.

When my mum said 'Thank you', Dennis said a weird thing. He said, 'She'd be sitting on my face if you weren't here.' This made Dennis's friend Martin laugh, but it didn't make me laugh, because I don't know why anyone would sit on someone's face. My mum told him to 'Shut up', so I think sitting on someone's face must be a bad thing. I think it would stop someone from breathing. It doesn't even make sense. Why would you want to sit on someone's face if they bought you a present? It means everyone would want to sit on Father Christmas's face instead of his knee, and then he would be dead.

Dennis always buys my mum presents when he has done something wrong. He even bought five bars of chocolate when he went to the shop. He normally just gets fags. Den's fags are called Regal King Size.

My mum has always wanted to learn to play guitar, so it made her happy in a way, even though I could spot some leftover sadness in her eyes. I was not happy that he was back, but I didn't say anything. I just did my drawing at the table, and then I watched *EastEnders* before I went to bed. *EastEnders* is my favourite programme. It's about a lot of people who live in London, and it's about all the bad things that happen to them. There was a man called Den on *EastEnders*, and he was horrible too. He was extra sly, the same as the Den that lives with us. Someone shot him because he was so bad. I bet all people called Den are nasty.

When I was in bed, I looked through my football cards and memorised the players and clubs. I could hear my mother learning to play the guitar. It didn't sound very good, but I think she will get better, because practice makes perfect. I think I would like to play guitar when I am older. Most of all, I just want to play football. I think if I try very hard I could be good enough to play for a team. I am playing football a lot, and I watch it when it's on the telly in the pub. I haven't decided which team to support yet, because there are so many, and I don't know which team to choose. I like the colours of the West Ham United team shirt, but I asked my mum where West Ham is, and she said it's in London, so it is too far to go and watch them play. Auntie Carol and Uncle Dave live in London, and one day we are going to go there to see them. Normally they come to see us, but it would be nice to go there for once.

TEACHERS

Today it was parent's day. It should be called parent's night, because my mum went to the school in the nighttime. She had to see Mrs R about my work, and I had to stay with Den. When she came home, I could tell that she was not happy about something. I was shocked because I had done all the work right, and I had done extra work that was supposed to be for the next class up. Mrs R lets me do it if I haven't got any more work to do. She said I can do some work which is meant to be for ten-year-olds. That is extra clever because I am only seven and a half.

This is what my mum said. My work is very good, but I have to write new, different stories in school.

I said, 'Why?'

She said, 'Because we talked about this, and I told you, you won't be able to watch films with Grandad if you keep writing about vampires and monsters and killing people.'

My teacher is stupid about stories. She forgets that they are fiction, even though she taught us what fiction is. She goes mad if you kill someone in a story, but that is stupid, because all the good stories and films I have seen have got dead people in them. Anyway, it's not like you've killed someone in real life – you're only doing it in your imagination or on paper. You can't really murder someone in a schoolbook. Sometimes teachers are ridiculous.

Mrs R showed my mum my story about vampires killing Dennis. I drew a picture to go with it. I tried really hard to get it right. It was a vampire biting Dennis's face off. My mum said she laughed when she saw it, but Mrs R didn't think it was very funny. Then I didn't say anything, because Den walked into the room. My mum didn't say anything in front of him, either.

At bedtime my mum read my sister a story called *The Golden Goose*. I was in my bed and just listening and looking at the ceiling stars. When she came over to tuck me in, she stroked my fringe and said, 'Do you remember doing the "When I Grow Up" topic in school?'

'Yes,' I said.

She kept stroking my hair.

'Do you remember what you wrote?'

'Yes.'

'Why did you write those things?'

I told her that I wrote them because they are true, and that means they are the right answers to the questions.

Mrs R always says I'm clever, and then she moans about my work. It doesn't make any sense. My mum went quiet, and her eyes looked even bluer than normal. She kissed me and said, 'OK. Night, night, watch the bed bugs don't bite.' Then she turned my lamp off, but she left the landing light on just in case we got scared.

THIS IS THE WORK SHE WAS TALKING ABOUT:

EXERCISE: WHEN I GROW UP:

Jack wants to be a milkman.
Jill wants to be a teacher.
Eric wants to be a fireman.

WHAT DO YOU WANT TO BE?

A scientist, a footballer and a fixed man.

Jack wants to go to America.
Jill wants to go to Australia.
Eric wants to go to Japan.

YOU CAN GO ANYWHERE. WHERE WOULD YOU LIKE TO GO?

Into the right body. Also, on holiday to Canada.

I couldn't sleep because I was worried about parent's day. School is confusing sometimes. I made a list of the things I like and don't like about it to try to make my brain more comfy.

THINGS I LIKE ABOUT SCHOOL:

- School dinners (especially 'afters', when we have cake and custard). Sometimes, after dinner, when we are playing in the yard, the dinner lady rings the school bell and shouts 'seconds', and me and Michael go back in to have a second dinner. It is only going in the bin, so it is OK for us to have it. Otherwise, it would just be a waste. It's a shame they can't send all the leftover food to poorer countries, because then nobody would have to starve.
- When we sing (We All Live in a) 'Yellow Submarine' every morning in assembly. The song is a lie, because we don't live in a submarine. It does rain a lot, and sometimes you feel like you live underwater, because everything is always wet. We don't live in a yellow submarine, though. We live in a country called Wales, in a valley between mountains. We also live in council houses. I like the song. It sounds extra nice, but doesn't make any sense.
- Story time – when we can choose our own book from the library.
- Free time – when we can choose an activity to do.
- Science – when we learn about space.
- English – when we are allowed to make up our own stories (and I don't get told off for killing people in my imagination).
- Playtime – when we play football in the yard, and I am the goalie and pretend I am Les Sealey.

THINGS I DON'T LIKE ABOUT SCHOOL:

- When I have to wear my nemesis the skirt, and I feel very stupid and sad.
- When some of the other kids say I am a girl or a tomboy. A tomboy is a girl who doesn't like skirts or lipstick. It doesn't mean you're a wrong boy, though. I'm not a tomboy.
- When I am not allowed to play football in PE.
- When the teacher says I have to do disgusting gymnastics instead of football.
- When teachers don't make any sense.
- Being late and having a row.

Mrs R doesn't give us bad rows, but in my old class the teacher used to go berserk if I was late. She used to poke me in the collarbone with her crooked witch fingers. I used to be scared if I heard the bell ring on my way to school.

Then, one day when we were late, my mum took me into the class, and when she went the teacher did it again. I didn't know, but my mum was watching through the glass part of the door, and she saw her do it. She went nuts. She burst into the class and said, 'Get your hands off her, you bitch. If you ever touch her again, I'll fucking kill you.'

My mum hardly ever swears, so it was a shock. All my friends had goldfish-style faces. Michael's face was the funniest. His mouth was a massive O. My mum didn't kill the teacher, though. Instead, the headmistress took her into the office and gave her coffee, and then she cried. I know because I had to go with her. Witch-bones never did it again, though. I think people get scared if you say you'll kill them, even if you don't mean it.

DOORSTEP

My dad didn't turn up when he was supposed to. I thought he was just late, so I sat on the doorstep and waited for him. My mum kept telling me to come in because it was getting very cold, but I wouldn't listen. I had my coat on, and my rucksack was on my back. I put it on to save time, so I would be ready to go when he turned up. My dad is always late. It's just normal for him. He doesn't wear a watch, and I think he should. I will ask my mum to buy him one for Christmas. It will be a present from me, not my mum.

It was very cold, my mum was right, but I didn't want to go in because it felt like I would be giving up on my dad. I watched the sky getting darker – it went blue, navy, purple. My mum kept saying 'He's not coming' and 'Come inside please', but I kept looking at the end of the street and waiting for my dad to walk around the corner. He didn't.

I had to go in because my mum was going nuts and I was freezing. Then I cried. Not because I was cold, but because I was sad that my dad wasn't there. Then my mum started shouting and saying nasty things about him, and it made me even sadder. She said, 'He's a useless, selfish bastard.' So we had another row.

My dad made everyone mad because he didn't do what he said he would do. I wondered if my dad was mad, and that's why he didn't turn up. I think his team lost the game. And I think he was drunk, and I think he forgot, because when you are drunk you do not understand things properly, and you forget to do things that matter. You can even forget you were supposed to pick your kid up. When I am older, I am only going to have one pint of lager on a Saturday. I don't think you would forget anything after one pint. One pint is probably safe for your brain.

COUSIN

Today was good because I saw my cousin Stefanie. She is my best cousin and she is 18. She is called my second cousin, and she is on my dad's side. She was visiting my next-door neighbour (Gill) and my mum at the same time. When I'm older, I want to marry her, because I love her, and she is the prettiest person I have ever seen that is not from a film. She is even more beautiful than Sigourney Weaver (the real person who acts as Dana Barrett in *Ghostbusters*). She has got the same hairstyle, too.

Sometimes, when I am out in the street playing, I do a test on myself. I try to run to the end of the street before I can count to ten. If I can do it, it means I will be able to marry Stefanie when I am older. I always lose, though.

I think Stef might want to marry me, because she is always complaining to Gill about her boyfriend and saying that he's bad. I wouldn't be bad. I would be good. I will also have the right clothes and hair to make me look smart when I am older. The other reasons she might like to marry me are because I haven't got a nasty face and I already love her more than I love football. When you love someone properly, it means you would rather get run over than watch it happen to them. It means you wish they would win a million pound more than you wish you would win it. It means you would give them your last Rolo, or even all of your Rolos, if they were hungry. It means you still like to look at their face even if there is something really good on the telly. I love loads of people properly. Most of them are in my family. I love Stef, even though I don't see her that much.

DRACULA

We were allowed to write ghost stories in school because of Hallowe'en. That means Mrs R is very stupid, because she said I wasn't supposed to write them and then she told me to do it. I wrote about Dracula. I know about Dracula because I have seen him in a film. I'm not supposed to watch old people's films because of what happened when I saw it. It was ages ago and I was only six then, so it wasn't my fault.

I was staying with Grandad, and we were looking for a film to watch. I picked up *Dracula* and he said, 'No, you can't watch that.' Then I told a small white lie and said I had seen it before. I liked the sound of the word D-R-A-C-U-L-A. It sounded extra interesting. I couldn't see what it would be like because there was no picture on the cover because it was on a tape called Scotch. It had a white sticky label with Grandad's writing, which meant he nicked it off the telly. Grandad let me watch it with him. I don't know if he believed the lie, though.

I sat in the brown armchair and Grandad lay in his spot on the floor right in front of the telly. He was lying sideways, so I could only see the back of his head, not his face. He always lies like that. I think it is so he can see and hear everything properly.

Dracula wasn't scary in the beginning. The music was, but I wasn't even scared. It was just people talking for ages and walking around. I was very shocked when Dracula (the man in black clothes) tried to eat a lady. I jumped and screamed and hid my face behind a cushion. Grandad must have got scared because he shouted, 'What the bloody hell!' and then he made the telly do a giant hiss noise. It sounded like a million snakes.

I was still scared, but I opened my eyes anyway, because I knew Dracula was gone. Grandad's hair had all flicked forward, and he was trying to get the telly to go back to normal, but it was just black with white snow. He kept saying, 'Jesus Christ!' and 'For goodness' sake!' I think I scared him by screaming. I don't think he was scared by the film, because he has seen it before. When the telly was showing the news, he said, 'You said you'd seen it,' and 'It's all right, it's all right now.' Then he put all his things back where they belonged, because he had tipped the ashtray over, and there was fag ash all over the carpet.

When my nan came home from work, she found out about Dracula and told Grandad off. She said he mustn't let me watch old people's films. He didn't listen, though. He just explained about Dracula being a vampire, and then it wasn't that scary any more. It's not scary, it's just horror, but now Grandad tells me what films are about before we watch them, just in case.

HALLOWE'EN

Hallowe'en is one of my favourite days because I am allowed to wear good clothes. I decided to dress up as Dracula because he looks extra smart, and I love him even though he used to scare me. Also, vampires have much better hair than zombies or ghosts. It's just the rules.

My mum made my costume out of old black clothes, and I used a black bag for a cape. She bought me a pair of plastic fangs from the little shop, too. I was allowed to gel my hair back, and I had my face painted with special white powder. My mum dressed up as a witch. She painted her face with green food colouring, and she wore a black bag too. The food colouring is meant for cakes, but my mum said it wouldn't hurt to use a bit on her face. Even though my mum is pretty, she looked scary. My sister had her normal clothes on, and a mask, but she looked quite evil when we put her in the buggy. She can walk, but sometimes she gets tired, so my mum still lets her go in it.

We all went trick-or-treating, and we went to loads of houses. Nearly everyone answered. Ricky gave us all his spare change, and Gary (Michael's uncle) gave us Love Hearts and loads of chocolate. We got a whole carrier bag full of sweets. When I got home, I tipped my bag on to the carpet and counted everything out. I had a one-pound coin, two fifty-pence pieces and loads of coppers. I had lots of chocolate and sweets, too. That wasn't even the best part of Hallowe'en, though. The best part was my mum invited Auntie Sandra and Luke over for tea, and we had beef burgers and chips. Then me and Luke ate loads of sweets and played, and they didn't go home till it was very late. Auntie Sandra is my most special auntie. I haven't told anyone she's my best one, but my heart knows she is. I felt very happy when it was Hallowe'en and they were here. I preferred being Dracula to being myself, anyway. I had a much better time being him.

GRANCHA

My dad turned up out of the blue. Out of the blue means you weren't expecting it. He took me to my grancha's house for tea. I hadn't been there for ages, so it was nice to see him.

Grancha is supposed to live with my nan B, but he doesn't because he decided he didn't like her. If you don't like the lady you marry, you have to have a divorce. Now he lives in a house on top of the mountain with a different woman who has got drawn-on eyebrows in the shape of upside-down Vs. I think he likes her more than my nan, even though her eyebrows make her look like a vampire. It's OK, though, because my nan lives with a new person too. She lives with a man called Ted, who has got big gold rings on his fingers and an accent like the people on *EastEnders*. I think my nan prefers Ted to my real grancha. I am glad my nan has got a new husband, because I wouldn't want her to be lonely.

Families are confusing, especially when everyone breaks up. I still think people should have better checks for deciding who they like before they get married. If I ever get married, I am going to do loads of tests on the woman to check I like her. The main thing I will check is if she has got brown curly hair, because brown curly hair is my favourite for girls. I would also check if she likes dogs and has got kindness in her eyeballs. You can always tell if people have got kindness in them, because it leaks from their eyes. Sometimes it is quite hard to work out if people are kind, because some people have other things inside their eyes too, like sadness or worry, but if they are kind, you will see it if you look hard, because kindness shines brighter than anything else. Another way you can tell about kindness is if you hold someone's hand. If they are kind, you can feel it on their fingers. I think it drips out of their skin.

I only hold my mum's hand and my dad's hand, and sometimes Stef's, and my little sister's. You mustn't hold hands with strangers. My mum has got cold hands that feel like paper. My favourite thing to do is look at her veins. I do it when we are on the bus or the train. My mum's veins are big, and it always looks like they are going to burst open. Sometimes I push them down with my finger and watch them bounce back up. I only do it gently. My mum thinks it is a silly habit, but I can tell that she doesn't mind.

Inside Grancha's house, there is a big painting on the wall. Inside the painting, there is a lady with no clothes on and a man with no clothes on. The man is standing on a swan's wing. It's very odd. There are lots of little gold horses on the shelves, and there is a fire which works by burning coal. Coal comes from under the ground in a coal-mine. There's loads of it in Wales. We learnt about it in school. My dad said there was a big row about coal because some people wanted to keep getting coal out of the ground, and some people said it's too dangerous. He said, 'It's that fucking witch Maggie's fault.' My dad gets angry about coal, but I think coal feels nice and cosy.

I like it when we go to Grancha's because we always watch Laurel and Hardy before my dad brings me home. This time we watched a Laurel and Hardy film called *Brats*. It was very funny. Laurel and Hardy is one of my favourites. I went home after *Bullseye*. *Bullseye* is one of my dad's favourites. I think it is OK, but some of the prizes are quite stupid, like plates or a suitcase or a gold clock. You can win a speedboat if you are extra good at darts, though.

SCREAM

In the middle of the night I could hear screaming. I had a horrible feeling in my stomach, because when I was properly awake I knew that the scream belonged to my mum. I ran out of my room to see what was wrong and I saw Dennis. He was pulling her down the stairs by her hair. She was on the floor, so he couldn't pull her far. She was telling me to go back to my room, but I didn't because I wanted to help her. I shouted at him to stop, but he was being extra crazy, and he wouldn't listen. Then he kicked her, and it made me so mad that I jumped on his back and tried to hit him. I'm not very strong, so he just pushed me off, and I felt like I was very rubbish because I couldn't help.

Then I had to stop thinking about my mum because I could hear my sister crying. She was just stood on the landing watching. Her cry made me feel very strange, because it is not nice to see a little girl crying because something terrible like that is happening. I took her back into our room and got into bed with her and sang her a song to try to cover up the noise. I also lied and said that they were just playing a game. I don't know which thing made me feel worse – my mum getting hit or my sister being scared. I sang 'Dream' off Mum's *Golden Oldies* tape, because it is my sister's favourite song. And I wanted her to go to sleep and dream so she would be having a nice time, even if it was a lie and it was not really happening.

RAMBO

My mum has got a black eye. I saw it this morning before she put her make-up on. It made me very sad and angry. I feel extra sorry for my mum all the time. I wish I could help her. You couldn't tell that she had a black eye when we went out of the house, because the make-up is like beige-coloured camouflage. Camouflage is a hard word. I had to look in my dictionary to spell it. It was even hard to find the word, because I was guessing the letters wrong.

Camouflage is what Rambo wears to hide in the jungle, and soldiers wear it to try to hide from their enemies. My mum is not wearing camouflage to hide from the enemy. She is wearing it so that people don't know about Dennis hitting her. Some people know, though. My dad knows, and my auntie Gail knows – I heard them talking about it before – but some people cannot see through camouflage. My mum is a bit like Rambo when he seems invisible in the jungle. I watched *Rambo* with Grandad, but I prefer *Rocky*. It is much more exciting. Getting hit by a bully is not exciting. It is terrible. I felt extra sorry for my mum because when we walked up the shop to get some milk she looked like a sad ghost lady. I think it is because being sad makes a bit of you fade and disappear.

CATS

I woke up because I could hear a horrible sound. It was my mum, but this time she was doing a different type of screaming. It didn't make me feel the way the 'on the stairs' screaming made me feel, but it made me feel strange. The feeling landed in my stomach. It was the nasty butterflies that tell you something's wrong. The sound was coming from my mum's bedroom, so it was very loud, because her bedroom is right next door to mine, and the wall is quite thin. It is not a proper brick wall. It is called plasterboard.

The noise was terrible, and it sounded the same as the cats in our street who sometimes mate in the night-time. Mrs R taught us about mating in our science lesson. It is when animals make babies. I think my mum was doing mating, but I think it is a very bad idea, because Den is horrible to her, so I don't understand why she would want to have another baby with him. I pulled the quilt over my head and said (out loud) all the players and teams I have learnt off by heart from my football cards. I did it to hide the sound. The sound made me feel sick, and it put me in a bad mood and upset me, but I didn't really know why.

STUPID

I have found out that you are not allowed to marry your cousin. This news made me feel very sad and stupid for thinking I could do it in the first place. I found out when I was talking to my mum about getting married when I am older. She explained that cousins don't match so they mustn't mate. If cousins have babies together, the babies could be ill. It's the same as dogs when they have a litter of weak puppies with rubbish legs. I don't want to do mating, and I don't want to have babies. The sound of mating makes me feel very red.

I think the cousin rule is a very stupid rule because Stefanie is my cousin, and that means I already know her well, and I have checked that I love her properly. Anyway, you can't break up from cousins. Cousins are for life, not just until you get fed up with them. Even if they get on your nerves, they're still yours. I also found out that I won't be allowed to marry her because of the girl problem, even though it is a lie. I won't be allowed to marry her because of the mistake, because a girl and a girl are not allowed to marry each other. I think this is also a stupid rule, because you should be allowed to marry whoever you want as long as you love them properly and you treat them softly and don't kick them in the stomach or drag them down the stairs by their hair. I hope they change the rules when it's my turn to get married. I bet they will, especially if Margaret Thatcher is dead and there's a new, kinder Prime Minister.

GUY FAWKES

We learnt about Guy Fawkes and the Gunpowder Plot today. Mrs R said a gang of men planned to blow up the Houses of Parliament in London. They planned it so that they could kill the King, and also because they didn't like some of the laws that were made there. Guy Fawkes got caught in the cellar under Parliament with 36 barrels of gunpowder. He didn't set it on fire, though. I think he might have changed his mind about doing it, or maybe the plan went wrong, but he still got tortured and killed. I don't think that is very fair, because he wasn't the only one in on the plan, and he didn't get around to lighting the gunpowder. It is like Michael stealing a load of Mars bars from the shop and me standing by them and thinking about eating one. I don't think we would get killed for that.

Mrs R said we celebrate the failed Gunpowder Plot because we are remembering that the King was not killed, and Parliament was not ruined. She said that is why we throw Guy dolls on to bonfires on Bonfire Night. I think all dolls should be thrown on the fire, except Cabbage Patch dolls. They're not too bad. I also think Guy Fawkes wasn't a real villain. When I told Mrs R that I felt sorry for Guy, she told me not to write that in my neat book, so I wrote it in this green book instead.

BONFIRE NIGHT

In the field by my house there was a giant bonfire. Ricky (from the next street) built the bonfire out of all the junk that people didn't want any more. The junk had to be stuff that would burn, though, like cupboards and other wooden things. Ricky was in charge of lighting it and setting off the fireworks. Michael's uncle Gary gave out free sparklers and hotdogs, which was extra nice of him.

Even though we were stood by a big fire, it was still very cold. Verity kept putting her hands over her ears because the fireworks were scaring her, so I let her wear my earmuffs, and then she was OK. My favourite fireworks are rockets. I don't think my mum likes fireworks very much, because she kept jumping when they made a noise. She still let us stay until the end, though.

Everyone from our street was out. Michael was there with all of his family except the dogs. It was extra fun, especially when we were playing with the sparklers. We had a race to write our names in the air. They disappeared too quickly, though.

When we went home, my hands were tingling because I was cold, and it was nice and cosy inside. As soon as we got in, my sister fell asleep, so my mum put her to bed, but she let me stay up late with her. Dennis wasn't in. He is out all the time lately. I wish he would STAY OUT FOR GOOD.

BMX

I was riding my bike in the street, and two big girls came up to me. They were nagging me to let them have a turn. One was fat with straight hair, and one was very tall with curly hair. I didn't know them. The extra-tall one kept saying, 'Come on, give us a go.' I told them I'm not allowed to lend my bike to anyone, but they just kept asking and saying, 'Only to the end of the street.' I said no, but one girl stood in front of me, and the other one stood behind me. They blocked me so I couldn't move. Then the tall girl climbed on by bike, even though I was still sat on it, and the fat girl pulled me backwards, so I fell off. Then I just had to wait to get it back.

She was riding it for ages. She kept going slow and pretending to stop and then riding off really fast. Every time I got near her she rode away again. They were both laughing. She kept doing it for a long time, so I said, 'Please give it back,' but she wouldn't. Then I tried to take it off her, but she pushed me and said, 'It's mine now.' It was a stupid thing to say because my bike is much too small for her because I am only little. I don't know how old the girl is, but I think she is in comp.

I ran home and told my mum because I was so angry I was nearly crying. My mum was washing dishes and looking out of the front window, which meant she could see the girls in the street. I said, 'Mum, those big girls are stealing my bike. They won't give it back,' but my mum didn't answer. She just kept washing a plate for ages. I kept asking her to go and tell them, but she just stared out of the window like a zombie with marble eyes. You always see zombies in films, but I have never seen one washing a plate and staring out of a window. It was very strange to see my mum like that, and I couldn't understand why she wouldn't help me.

I went back outside and tried to get the bike back by myself, but the girl was too strong. She tried to pull my hand off the handlebar, but I wouldn't let go. I only let go in the end because she pushed me really hard and I fell. Then I grabbed on to the back wheel and wrapped both my hands around it and hung on for as long as I could. I was lying on the pavement, and she started to ride away, and I was worried I would get dragged down the street or get my hand trapped under the wheel. It was really hurting, too, so I had to let go.

They were going away, and I just had to watch them. They were both laughing. I sat on the pavement, and I felt the tears burning my eyeballs. When they went into the next street, I cried. I couldn't believe they would steal my bike, and I couldn't understand why my mum didn't do anything to help me. I sat on the wall and cried for ages. I didn't stop crying even when the lampposts pinged and turned orange.

FIRE

When I woke up, I got dressed and went out to look for my bike. I didn't even wake my mum up. I think she was still tired from being a zombie, anyway, so I just went out. I am supposed to tell her first, but I was too angry to care about the rules. I went all around the street and the back lanes, and then I walked through the field. I was looking for ages. I even went down by the river, even though I'm not meant to. I did it quickly, and I kept checking behind me for strangers. I always look out for strangers when I'm on my own. There wasn't anything down by the river, only an old tyre and a trolley sticking out of the water. The handlebar said Carrefour.

I walked back through the field, and I saw something shiny in the distance, so I ran to check it. When I got close to it, I knew it was my bike, but it didn't look like it any more. It was in the ashes of the bonfire, and the tyres were burnt off. I think the girls who stole it had tried to burn it, which is very stupid because my bike is made of steel, and everyone knows steel doesn't burn properly unless the fire is extra hot like a volcano. I think they just threw it in the bonfire because they were bored of it. They got bored of my bike because the fun part was taking it off me. I didn't touch it, because even though the fire was out and dead, I didn't know if something could still burn me.

I said goodbye to my bike, which was a stupid thing to do, because my bike is an object, and objects don't have feelings or say goodbye like humans. I still said it, though. I said sorry for losing it, too. And I called the big girls an ugly daddy-long-legs and a fat fucking beach ball. I said it quietly, and then I ran back to the street.

Even though I was still sad, I decided to stay out and play. I played football in the street for most of the day because it made me happier, and every time I kicked the ball, a bit of the sad bike feeling got left behind in the gravel. Gravel is when the street breaks into tiny pieces.

I was playing on my own for ages, and then Michael came out, and we played 5 Alive against the wall. I told him all about the girls and my bike.

'They are so nasty,' I said. 'I would never steal a bike off a little kid if I was in comp.'

'Don't worry,' Michael said. 'They're just bastards. You can have a go on my bike every day if you want. I don't mind sharing.' Michael's bike is quite old, but it still works properly. It's just a bit rusty.

I went home and watched telly, then I had cheese and potato pie for tea and a packet of salt-and-vinegar crisps and a Classic. My mum just had jelly. She didn't even say anything about my bike. It felt like she didn't care, or notice. She was still half zombie anyway.

BULLIES

When we were having dinner in the hall, some kids from the big class were making fun of Lucy. They wouldn't sit by her, and they moved on to another table. Then they were laughing and whispering, and they called her a spaz and a mong. It was because some of the custard she was eating was falling out of the sides of her lips. I didn't laugh. Neither did Michael. We went to sit by her to keep her company, because it is not nice to have dinner on your own. I don't care that Lucy eats in a funny way, and I don't care about things like someone dribbling custard.

Lucy is nice. I feel sad for her because sometimes people stare at her, even though it is rude, and they should have better manners. My mum said Lucy is handicapped. It means she's got something wrong with her, but I don't know exactly what it is. It's obvious, though. You can see it in the style of her eyes, and her mouth and the way she speaks. Also, one of her legs is too lazy and it sticks out, so she's all stiff like a Barbie doll. Lucy is lovely. She's not a spaz, she's just different. You should never be nasty to people because they are different. Those kids are just bullies, like Dennis and the girls who took my bike.

You can tell if there is something wrong with most people just by looking at them. For example, if you see someone and they're in a wheelchair, or they haven't got any legs, you know they can't play football. Or if you see someone with no arms, you wouldn't ask them to play tennis or pool or anything like that. You can't really tell by looking at me that there's something wrong, though. You wouldn't spot it unless you are extra clever. Mrs R is only clever with fractions. I have decided not to ask her for help with my mystery.

THE WALL

On the way home (from his house) my dad did the strangers talk again. He tells me about strangers every time I see him. I think he forgets he has already said it all before. He does it like a test, but I already know all the answers. *Don't have a lift or an ice-cream from a stranger. Don't let anyone touch my privates. Always tell my mum where I'm going.* Then he said, 'I know Dennis hurts your mother, but if he ever hurts you, I want you to tell me, OK?' Every time my dad asks me if Dennis has done anything bad to me, I want to lie and say yes. I always want to say he has done something because I hate Dennis, and I want him to go away. I don't, though, because that would be bad, and it would also be a lie, but this time when my dad asked me, I said, 'Yes,' because it was the truth.

Dennis doesn't normally hurt me, except by hurting my mum, but on Tuesday, when my mum was out, he went mad. At first, he was OK. He was lifting his weights, and he only stopped to rub white powder on his gums. I think it is special weight-training medicine that makes you stronger. Then he started shouting for no reason, and he had dead eyes.

I went up into my room to play, but when he came upstairs to go to the toilet, he started shouting at me and told me to clean my fucking room. Then he picked me up and threw me at the wall. It didn't hurt much because of the plasterboard, and I landed on my bed, so it was a soft landing. It made me sad, though, because I didn't do anything to deserve it. It also made me sad, because I don't think you are supposed to throw kids at the wall, especially if the kid is not your kid.

When I told my dad, he went a funny dark red colour, and his eyes turned black like two lumps of coal. He started walking extra fast. I had to run to keep up with him. When we got to my house, he banged on the door and was shouting for Dennis to come outside. My mum answered the door and said Dennis wasn't in. My dad said, 'Tell that fucking cunt I'm gonna kill him.' I am not supposed to say that word. Cunt. I don't say it. I don't even know what it means. I think it means nasty person, so it is the right word for Dennis. He is a cunt. I won't ever say it, though, because it is a swear word. I don't think I am allowed to write it down either, but I don't care because this is my book, and that means I can write whatever I want in it. Dennis is a cunt. Cunt. Cunt. Cunt.

FATHER CHRISTMAS

There was a Christmas party in the church hall. I went with my dad. Everyone was there, even Stefanie. There were sandwiches and normal party food, and there was also Christmas food like mince pies and Christmas cake. Father Christmas visited at the end of the party because it is almost Christmastime, and sometimes he just does things like that to surprise you.

At the party, I was wearing my cream Christmas jumper and red tracksuit bottoms. My Christmas jumper has got a holly pattern and a giant Christmas pudding in the middle. When we went shopping, there was a grey Christmas jumper with a reindeer pattern, and I wasn't allowed to have it because it was for a normal boy. I really wanted it because I liked the pattern. A Christmas pudding is OK, though, I suppose. My clothes felt nice and soft, and I was comfortable, so I could play properly. I was glad I didn't have to wear a stupid Christmas dress like Jodie's. She looked like a Christmas cracker.

Father Christmas sat on the stage, and everybody else was sitting in the hall, looking up at him. He said, 'Ho, ho, ho, merry Christmas!' Then everybody else said, 'Merry Christmas!' at the same time, like in school when a teacher says, 'Good morning, class,' and we all say it back. We didn't have to say 'Merry Christmas' in Welsh as well, though.

'Have you all been good boys and girls?'

Everybody was shouting yes, even the grown-ups. I thought I had been quite good, apart from telling the Indian lie. Father Christmas called out kids who had been put on the *good* list and told them to go up on to the stage to collect a present. Jodie was first, and when she came back to her chair, she opened her present straight away. It was a doll set with clothes and shoes. It looked rubbish, but she liked it.

Then he said, 'Is there a little boy called Kai here?' Kai smiled and pointed at himself. He had a bubble-gun present, which just fired water bubbles, so it was OK for him to have, because it wasn't dangerous. I started to feel a bit worried about it being my turn, even though I did want to get a new toy.

Next it was Aaron's turn. He had a marble set, and the marbles inside it were called Frenchies. Lots of kids had their turn before me, and some of the presents were good ones. I hoped I would get the same present as Aaron so we could play each other (for keeps).

When it was my turn Father Christmas said two things that made me feel red and hot. He said, 'Do we have a little girl called...' Then he said my real name – the shade of green, not the name Green. The words made my face burn because I knew I had to stand up and say 'yes', but I didn't want to. I didn't say anything, so my auntie said, 'Yes, over here,' and I had to walk up in front of everyone to collect my present. I said, 'Thank you,' and sat back down in my seat quickly.

When I felt my present, I could tell that it wasn't marbles. I ripped the snowflake paper off and stared at it. It was a book with a box of wool and needles. My present was called *Learn to Knit*. The knitting present made me feel mad, because all the other boys had cars or guns or trucks or marbles, and I had a present that taught you how to make a scarf. I tried not to be angry because when someone gives you a present, you are supposed to be happy, even if you didn't want it. If you're not, you're being ungrateful. I didn't want to be ungrateful, but I didn't want to do stupid knitting either. My nan does knitting, and knitting is for girls, especially old girls. Old women love knitting. They think it is a good hobby, but it isn't. I wouldn't want to do knitting even if I was one hundred and two years old. I hated Father Christmas because of the knitting present, and that made me feel very sad and confused because I used to love him. I just want him to know I'm a boy.

LETTER

Mrs R told us to write a letter to Father Christmas. When I said it was a bit late because it is nearly Christmastime, she told me to be quiet, and then she said, 'Just listen for once, please.' She said that Father Christmas is magic, so 'don't worry about it'. I just did as I was told, because sometimes Mrs R gets annoyed when you ask lots of questions. I had to help Michael with his letter because he was stuck on some spellings. Michael wanted some new transformers. He used to have Optimus Prime, but his brother accidentally broke it. I don't know if you can ask Father Christmas for the same present you've asked for before, but he did anyway. I couldn't spell Optimus Prime, so Mrs R helped. I only got one letter wrong. I put an A instead of an I. Michael also wanted a new BMX because his is getting old and it used to be his brother's. I want one, too. After I helped Michael I was quite bored, so I wrote my letter, even though I didn't want to.

Dear Father Christmas,

It feels funny writing to you, because I have started to think you might not be real. The only reason I think you must be real is because my mum has never got enough money, so I don't think she could afford to buy me presents and pretend they are from you. I will try to think you are real so I can write you a good letter. If you are real, I am sorry for saying that you aren't. If you are real, I also think you are very clever (in some ways).

I saw you at the Christmas party the other day, and you gave me a 'learn how to knit' set. I hope you don't think I am rude, but I want you to know that this is a very silly present for me because I am a boy, and I don't ever want to knit. I don't even understand why any real girls would want to knit, because knitting is boring, and you would never want to do it even if you were a hundred and you were bored of waiting for it to be your turn to die. I think knitting is boring, even if you are almost dead. I understand why you gave it to me, though. It is because I am on the girl list even though that is WRONG.

I don't know what to write because I don't think you ever get my letters. If you do get them, I don't know why you keep bringing me presents that I don't ask for. I think it is because my letter goes into the girl pile of letters. Or maybe your elves are reading them and getting things wrong. Last year I asked for Ghostbusters figures, and I got Barbie dolls. I shouldn't tell you this, in case you put me on the naughty list, but I want you to know. You probably already know anyway (if you are magic). I cut all the Barbie dolls' hair off and broke their legs because I hated them. I also stabbed one in the eye with my scissors. I'm not even sorry about it, because it made me feel better.

This year I would like:
- *A new BMX (because mine was stolen by two evil girls who don't deserve anything. They should be put on the naughty list for ever.)*
- *A leather football (because the plastic ones from the little shop go flat after two days.)*
- *A train set.*
- *Ghostbusters figures (if I can only have one, can I please have Peter Venkman.)*
- *Something for my mum to make her happy.*
- *If you can only get one thing, please can I have a bike (any colour except pink.)*

Thanks.
From Green (Jade) Waters.

PS: My grandad said you can die if you eat too much, just like if you don't eat enough, so I wouldn't eat a mince pie from every house in the world if I were you. Plus, you are already too fat.

QUESTIONS:

I am confused about Father Christmas because of a few things. I asked my mum some questions about him, and she didn't really answer. When my mum doesn't answer properly, it means she is trying to run away from the question. She said, 'Don't say anything to Luke about Father Christmas.' It made me wonder if I was right about him. These are the questions I asked:

Is Father Christmas a time traveller? I asked this because I tried to add up how long it would take him to deliver presents to every country, and it would take a lot longer than one night. I added up all the countries I could think of, and I looked in my atlas for more countries, and then I tried to work out how far he would have to travel. I also tried to work out how many *good* children there are on his list. I did it the way Mrs R told us to work out problems, and then I wrote down my answer. The answer was time traveller. My mum laughed when I asked her about Father Christmas time travelling, and that made me think I was wrong. Working things out can be very confusing.

OTHER QUESTIONS I ASKED ABOUT
FATHER CHRISTMAS:

- Can he speak all the languages in the world, or does he have to get some things translated? Translated is when words are turned into a language you know. I know about it because Grandad has got a special dictionary that turns English words into French ones.

- Why are the elves with him so tall?
- Why is his beard pretend?
- If he is so busy, why is he wasting time in shops having his photograph taken with kids?
- Or is he sending actors or fake versions of himself to have photographs in shops?

I think he is, because he looks different in every photo. In one photo I had with him he has got blue eyes, and in another one he has got green eyes. When I told my dad, he said I was very observant. Observant just means noticing tiny things. I always notice things, even really small things, like one of my dad's ears sticks out more than the other one, and my mum's eyes go extra sparkly before she cries. This is observant. Lots of people aren't observant. Most people hardly notice anything. Sometimes I wish I could stop noticing, because my brain feels like it will explode because of all the tiny things that I see and all the questions that shout out over each other. That is why I like playing football, because it makes my brain go nice and quiet. When I am playing football, my brain doesn't care about anything apart from getting the ball into the goal.

MY LAST QUESTION ABOUT FATHER CHRISTMAS:

- If he can see everything and knows everything, why does he keep giving me girl toys? Having the wrong kind of toys for Christmas is worse than having none. It is just very bad teasing.

CHRISTMAS CARD

When I told my mum about writing a letter to Father Christmas, she told me to sit at the table and write my Christmas list. I said, 'I've already done it. I gave it to you ages ago,' but she told me to do it again in case I had forgotten anything. She gave me a catalogue to look for ideas. Verity sat next to me, and she turned straight to the girly toys. My mum circled the things she pointed to. Then she helped us do our Christmas cards for people in school. She wrote all Verity's and she helped me with the hard spellings. My mum said we have to give everyone in our classes a card, even if we don't play with them much. I gave the kids I don't play with much the holly cards, and I saved the snowman ones for Michael, Anthony, Louise and Lucy. My sister didn't care who got a holly or snowman card. She doesn't care about many things. I think it is because she's still little and she's only in nursery. My mum says we are like chalk and cheese. It is because I care about everything and notice all the things in the world. My mum says my sister is an 'easy' child. I think it must be because she doesn't ask too many questions, and she always does what she's told. I also think it means I am the 'hard' child. If one thing is easy and one thing is hard, that is an opposite.

BLOOD

When Dennis came home from the pub, his face was covered in blood. It looked like a vampire had tried to eat his face, just like in my picture, but I don't think it could have been that, because I don't think there are vampires in Wales. Mrs R said there aren't vampires anywhere, but I don't know if she is just saying that. When I asked my grandad, he said there are people who are a bit like vampires, and they like to eat people. They are called cannibals. I don't understand why anyone would want to eat a person, especially when there is so much nice food in the world, like sausage and chips and Mars bars and Sunday dinner.

Dennis was drunk, but he wasn't acting nasty. He just went straight to bed. I think someone beat him up because he was nasty when he was out. He doesn't normally act nasty outside. He is a very good actor. Lots of people think he is nice because he pretends. When Den's mum and dad come to visit, he even has a different voice and face. He's never evil when they're here. He pretends he is not a villain. A villain is just a posh word for a baddy. The Den from *EastEnders* did the same thing. All the people who knew him thought he was a nice man who worked in the pub, but really he did bad things.

The person who beat Den up must have seen what he's really like. I tried not to be glad, because it is not nice to see someone with blood all over them, but really I was thinking that he deserved it. It serves him right, because he's a bully, and everyone knows boys are not supposed to hit girls. Den knows, but he does it anyway. That is called bullying. It's also called evil.

SHEPHERDS AND ANGELS

Today we had to do the nativity concert in school, and I was very angry because I had to be a stupid angel. I hated it, and I didn't sing any of the carols because I felt very silly. I had to wear a piece of silver tinsel on a hairband on top of my head. It was supposed to be a halo. The rest of the costume was just a white sheet with a jagged line. I felt like a ghost, so I pretended that I was a ghost, and I wished I would get sucked up into a ghost trap. I didn't have any words to say, and I was glad about that. That was the only good thing.

I wanted a different part in the concert. I didn't want to be Joseph. I didn't even want to be an innkeeper or a wise man, because then I would have had lots of words to say. I just wanted to be a shepherd, but I wasn't allowed. Mrs R said I couldn't be a shepherd because I'm a girl. I kept asking, but she kept saying, 'No, no, no!' Anthony and Michael were shepherds, and they were allowed to wear striped clothes and tea towels on their heads, and they had special long sticks called canes. It's not fair. I was very angry with Anthony, even though it wasn't his fault.

His tea towel was brown and white, and someone had spilt tea on it. I wanted to pull it off his head. I didn't, though, because that would have been spiteful and nasty.

My mum was in the audience, and I could tell she was annoyed because I wasn't singing or smiling. I think I looked stupid and wrong because all the other angels were happy and singing, like Samantha and Louise and Natalie. Also, I don't think there was an angry angel who wished they were a shepherd when Jesus was born.

When it was home time, my mum said, 'Why didn't you sing?'

I told her that I was very annoyed because I wasn't allowed to be a shepherd.

'You were the only one not singing,' she said.

I said, 'I didn't want to sing because the nativity concert is bloody stupid.'

My mum laughed, but it wasn't funny. When I got home, I just watched *Neighbours* and ate my tea and played with my cars. Then it was time for bed, and I was glad because it was such a rubbish day, and I was happy it was over. Some days are just fucking horrible.

CHRISTMAS DAY

'It's Christmas! Come on sleepyhead, let's see if *he's* been.'

My mum was talking about Father Christmas, and she was very excited. I was excited because Christmas is supposed to be the best day of the year, and I was also excited because I was hoping for a train set or a bike or any good things. I had a good feeling, and I was hoping it was going to be the best Christmas. I was also happy because Dennis was not there. He went out on Christmas Eve and didn't come back.

The first present I found was the right shape to be a figure. I opened it extra quickly, and I found out it wasn't a Ghostbuster. It was a Barbie doll with extra clothes. I thought it might be a mistake and it might have been meant for my sister, but my mum was smiling at me, so I smiled back because it looked like she was thinking it was a good present, even though it wasn't.

I opened the next thing, and I could tell straight away that it wasn't going to be a train set. When I tore off a part of the wrapping paper, I knew that it was another girls' toy by the colours which were pink and purple. I didn't even want to carry on pulling the paper off, but I knew I had to. It was a girls' toy, which was a pink castle, to put pretend horses in. It would have been a good present if it was a normal castle with knights and weapons. The next present was a pink horse with blue hair. I put it next to the castle box and wished I could like it. I tried really hard to trick myself into it, but you can't make yourself like something if you don't, it's too hard. If Father Christmas is real, I think he should sack all of his elves because they are doing a terrible job.

My mum was helping Verity to open her presents, but she was also looking at me, so I was trying to smile, but I started to feel so sad it was hard to make my face go into a smile shape. I decided to keep trying because I had lots of presents left, and I thought some of them might be the right ones. I opened the present from my auntie Gail. It was a Cabbage Patch doll. I hate dolls, but this one was not as bad as dolls like Barbie, and also, it was a boy.

Cabbage Patch dolls have names, and mine was called Michael. It was wearing a grey jumper with blue numbers. The number was 31. I didn't hate the doll as much as I normally hate dolls, but I didn't really want it either. I think I am too old for dolls, and even if I was a girl, I wouldn't want a doll. Dolls are ridiculous and boring.

When I finished opening my presents, my eyes were stinging. I was too sad to hide it from my mum, so I cried. Then I felt bad for crying, and I tried to be happy again. I didn't tell my mum I was crying because I didn't get a bike or a train set, but I think she could tell. Mums are strange like that. They always know what you are crying about, even if you don't want to tell them. I had three presents which I liked. They were:

1. A set of felt-tip pens with a colouring book.
2. Roald Dahl books (Roald Dahl is an extra-good storyteller).
3. A Spirograph set (*A fascinating way to draw over a million marvellous designs*).

I also had a book called *The Human Body* from Dennis's mum and dad. (It looks quite good.)

I don't think my sister was very happy with her presents, either. All she did was play with a cardboard box that a toy came in. I think she liked the box more than any of her toys.

Christmas dinner was the best part of the day. It was really nice, especially the roast potatoes. After dinner I did colouring in and drew pictures and then I watched the telly with my mum and sister and had some of my selection box. I ate the Fudge and the Crunchie, but I gave the Curly Wurly to my mum because I felt bad about crying. On the telly, there was a film called *Crocodile Dundee*. It was about a man who is stronger than crocodiles. The man is only used to living in the jungle, and he goes to try out living in New York City. It is also about kissing a girl. It was quite crap, but it was better than watching a musical.

BOXING DAY

I went to my dad's house for Boxing Day. It is just fair, because my mum had me at her house on Christmas Day, and they have to share me because I am both of theirs. It was brilliant at my dad's. I played with Kai and Aaron for ages. Their new toys were wicked. They had a Knight Rider Scalextric, and we took it in turns to race. Aaron had a boxing punchball and gloves. It is like a real boxing bag, but instead of being on a hook it is a ball on a stand. When you punch it, it springs back. It was amazing. We took it in turns to see who could hit it the hardest.

Then my dad let us hit him with the gloves on. I did it to test how strong I am, but I felt a bit bad, even though I knew it wasn't hurting him.

In the afternoon, we watched *Star Wars: Return of the Jedi*, and we had loads of chocolate. I didn't even care that I have seen the film loads of times. I just loved being with my dad. I love my dad more than football, but I don't love him more than my mum, I love them the same amount. Loving my mum feels different to loving my dad, though. I think it is because I miss my dad more and I am with my mum all the time. I still wish they liked living together, but it's just tough luck.

THE HUMAN BODY

Today I read the *Human Body* book. At first, it was extra interesting. It had big pictures of all the parts of the body. On one page it showed the outside of each body part, and on the opposite page it showed the inside. Even though it looked disgusting it was brilliant. The brain and the heart were the best parts.

I was really enjoying the book. It only started to get on my nerves when I got to the pages about private parts. There was a picture of a boy and a picture of a girl with all their private parts named. Not the normal names like willy and wee-wee, the proper names for parts which are penis and testicles for boys and vagina for girls. Then it had close up pictures of the privates which were labelled and showed the insides and the outsides. It was quite disgusting to see the parts close up. They looked horrible.

I took the book up to the bathroom because I wanted to see which picture I matched up with. I got the little mirror from above the sink, and I put it on the floor. Then I took my clothes off to look at my private parts properly. The mirror showed them close up. I kept checking the book and the mirror, checking what I matched. I couldn't believe it. The truth was a disgusting vagina. That was my match. Even though I already knew I was stuck in the girl skin, at the same time, I couldn't believe it. It felt like someone had played a nasty trick on me. I used to think my willy was just too small, and it would grow one day and catch up with the rest of me, but now I know I just haven't got one at all. I know it won't grow – even if I pray every night and I'm extra good, it still won't happen.

I felt extra stupid for thinking I had a willy, but I am not stupid. I'm on the top table. I even know about gravity and space, but I thought I had a willy, and I've got an ugly, disgusting vagina. It's a fact. The book is evidence. I ripped out the page and crumpled it up, and I cried for ages because I was so sad about being all wrong. It's the worst thing that's ever happened to me. Having a vagina when you're a boy is worse than your mum and dad splitting up. It's worse than anything.

MICHAEL'S HOUSE

It was too cold to play outside. Even the cats looked frozen. Michael wanted to show me his Christmas presents, so I was allowed to go over to his house. I told him about the Michael doll and the wrong presents. He thought the Michael doll was funny, but he thought the wrong presents were stupid too. He didn't get a new bike, either, but he did get some extra-good presents. He got a new transformer called Bumblebee instead of Optimus Prime. It was quite good because you could change it into a car. Michael's favourite toy was a special surprise that he didn't even ask for. It was a set of cowboys and Indians in a special case. They are toys, but also models, so you have to be careful not to break them. I thought they were excellent, and I loved the colours that they had been painted. Michael loved them, but he still let me hold them and play with them. I was extra careful.

Next, we played cowboys and Indians – not with the figures, just by pretending. I was the Indian, even though I wasn't wearing the skirt. I'm always the Indian, because Michael likes guns more than bows and arrows, and I prefer to be an Indian, anyway. Mrs R taught us about Indians in school. I prefer them to cowboys because Indians were wise. The cowboys were bad and stole land from the Indians and tried to kill them all. Nasty bastards.

BROKEN WINDOW

Dennis threw a brick through my mum's bedroom window. It landed on her bed, and the glass spilt all over her pillow. It was lucky we were staying at my nan's because I think the brick would have landed on my mum's head and killed her if she was at home in bed. My mum was crying again. I think she is sad because she loves Dennis, but she knows that he is bad.

The man next door (Alan – Gill's husband) covered up the window with wood and special tape. He said, 'That'll do the trick for now, love.' Someone is coming to fix it with new glass tomorrow. I hope my mum does not let Dennis come back. I think she would be happier if she had a normal type of boyfriend who doesn't love smashing things. I think she should pick someone like Egon Spengler, because he is very sensible and behaves in a good way. I don't think Egon Spengler would ever pull a lady down the stairs by her hair. I don't think any of the Ghostbusters would, not even Venkman. Because the window was broken and my mum was scared, she slept in my room with me and my sister. It was nice and cosy to have her in there with us, even though she was in there for a sad reason.

Since Den broke the window, my mum has been ill and has only been eating jelly and toast. She stays in bed all the time, too. She has turned into a zombie again. It's Den's fault. The other day, Dennis's dad came to our house, and he took all Den's stuff. I heard him tell my mum that he will keep him away. This made me very happy, even though my mum was still sad.

My nan is coming to stay to help my mum. She said she is going to stay for the whole week. This made me happy too. Even though my mum was very sad, she said Dennis would not be coming back. I didn't believe her, because once she said Dennis had to go, but she was lying. She made him leave, and he even took all of his clothes in his gym bag, but when he went, she wrote him a note and made me take it to him when he was at the bus stop. I wanted to throw the note in the bin and pretend the bus had already gone, but I know it is wrong to lie, so I gave it to him, and he came back. My mum said that won't happen again. She said, 'This is the last straw.' I think she meant the last brick.

BAD

Another bad thing happened. Dennis tried to come into the house in the night, even though all the doors were locked. He was shouting and going nuts, and he kept saying he was going to kill us all. Then he climbed up the drainpipe. We were all watching, even Verity. My mum opened the window and told him to go away, but he didn't listen. He was like the wolf in the *Three Little Pigs* story. I think he was drunk, because he wasn't making any sense, and his words were coming out all strange. My nan started shouting at him. She said, 'Go away, you nuisance,' but she didn't have her false teeth in, so she sounded silly. She looked quite funny, too, because she still had pink rollers in her hair. She always sleeps with them in.

Then a police car came into the street. It had blue lights flashing, but it wasn't making a noise. When Den saw it, he fell down the pipe really quickly, but he landed on his feet and tried to run away. It was half funny and half scary.

The policemen caught him, though. I heard the first policeman's radio, which was a walkie-talkie, but I couldn't hear what he said to Den, and I didn't see him put the handcuffs on him. They put him in the police car, and one policeman stayed in the car, and one knocked the door to speak to my mum. They said they are coming back to talk to her again tomorrow.

When they went, Gill (from next door) came over. She told my mum that she phoned the police. Then she put the kettle on and made three cups of tea, even though it was the middle of the night and it isn't her house. I had to go back to bed and take my sister with me, but it felt comfy to hear them talking downstairs. My sister got into my bed even though I didn't invite her. I didn't mind, though. I was still worried about my mum, but I was glad Gill called the police on Dennis. He always thinks he can get away with being horrible, but the police are there to make sure horrible people don't do bad things to nice people. It's their job to stop evil bastards from killing people. It must be the hardest job in the world.

BLOCKED

The police came back. They told my mum to sign pieces of paper, and they said they are going to put a special rule on Dennis so he can't come to our house or near my mum. It means Den is blocked from us and has to stay away, or he will go to jail. It is extra-good news. They can do it because he keeps being nasty, and he is out of chances. They said he used to be nasty to his last girl-friend and she called the police too. My mum is listening to what the policemen said. I hope she doesn't let Den come back this time.

I don't think people like Den can ever turn nice, be-cause some people don't know how to be. They don't have any niceness inside them. It's like they have got a missing ingredient. I think it is extra sad for my sister because she has got a horrible dad. I am lucky to have a nice one. The only bad thing about my dad is he is always late. Being late is much better than being nasty, though.

1990

SCHOOL

We had to go back to school today. I was happy about seeing my friends, but I was sad about wearing the skirt again. I even cried and had a row with my mum before we left the house. The row happened because, at first, I wouldn't get dressed. I was sitting on the floor, and I wouldn't take my pyjamas off. I kept asking to wear a tracksuit, and she kept saying, 'You better get dressed, now!' and, 'Right, that's it, I'm going to have a word with your father.' She always says she will have a word with my father if I won't listen.

THINGS I SAID NOT TO WEAR IT:

1. It's too cold outside to have bald legs. (TRUE)
2. I could fall on ice and cut my knees. (TRUE)
3. I could catch a cold because of the cold. (NOT SURE)
4. It's too small. (FALSE/LIE)
5. It's broken. (FALSE/LIE)
6. Louise wears a tracksuit, and she is a real girl. (HALF TRUE – SHE WEARS ONE ON FRIDAYS)

I think I was extra sad about wearing the skirt because I didn't have to wear one on any day in the Christmas holidays. It made it harder to put it back on. I did it in the end, because we were late for school, and I didn't want to get into more trouble.

I had to make up a story to help me do it, so I made myself believe I was an Indian chief, and the skirt was my very special uniform, and I was the only boy wearing it because I was the leader of my tribe. It felt nice to imagine I was a real Indian. In my imagination, all of the other Indians are red, but I am green, and they think I am special, so they make me the chief of the tribe. I have got the best horse, and I get to ride at the front of the pack. I am the leader, and my feathers are magnificent. Being an Indian chief is much better than being a wrong boy.

I was very angry with my mum all day, but I tried not to show it, because she's getting better. She's eating normal food, not just jelly, and I want her to stay normal and not turn into a full zombie.

THE BEANO

My nan went back to Grandad and her flat because my mum is a lot better now. I went with her to keep her company (on the three buses). I also did it because I was allowed to stay for one night. My nan had to go home because she had to go back to work in the pub. I stayed in with Grandad. I didn't mind, because I have seen my nan a lot and I haven't seen him much.

Before my nan went to work, she gave me a carrier bag full of books. A lady from the pub gave them to her. The lady's son had grown up and didn't like to read them any more. I didn't look at them at first, but when Nan went, and Grandad had his opera music on, I was quite bored, so I had a look in the bag. The books were called *The Beano*. They were annuals. I had never heard of *The Beano* before. I started looking through them and reading, and I couldn't believe that nobody had told me about it. It was like finding a special world that I didn't know existed. When I started reading, I couldn't stop.

The Beano is the best thing ever invented. It's the best thing I've ever read. It's brilliant. I read a whole annual before I went to sleep. I read stories about Dennis the Menace, the Bash Street Kids, Roger the Dodger and Ball Boy. Dennis the Menace is my favourite character. He is the only Dennis I know who's nice. He gets into mischief, but it's only for a joke. He's not really bad. He just loves pranks.

I was so happy with the annuals I was even smiling at the same time as reading. It felt like I was going inside another world without moving or getting off the settee. I wished I lived in the Beano world, because everything there is good and life there has got the best colours. The colours made me feel all fuzzed inside. I am allowed to keep all the *Beano*s and take them home with me. *The Beano* is one of my new favourite things, but I still like football and *Ghostbusters*. I am so glad I found out about it. I am going to collect *The Beano* for ever, even when I am a man and I have got a nice wife and a smart moustache.

HEAVEN

When I woke up, Nan had already gone to church, so I had to have cereals for breakfast, because Grandad doesn't cook. My nan goes to church because she is a Christian, and that is where Christians go on Sundays. It means she loves Jesus and believes in heaven. She is going to heaven when she dies. My nan says you go to heaven if you're good, and if you're bad you go in the burning fire. The burning fire is just another way of saying hell. I think she is lying about the burning fire, though. I think she is just saying it to scare people and get people to behave. She always says it to Luke if he won't eat his food or he won't get dressed. I hate it when she says it because I think it is stupid to be sent into a fire just because you don't want to do something.

On the wall in Nan and Grandad's flat there is a picture of heaven and hell. It is called *THE BROAD AND THE NARROW WAY*. It shows one path that leads to heaven and one path that leads to hell. On the way to heaven, there are streams, rainbows and churches, but on the way to hell you can fight, drink beer and ride a horse. The road to hell looks like much more fun, but it's no fun when you get there. When you get to hell, demons want to drag you into a fire.

It would be much cosier to believe in the Jesus story and all the stories in the Bible than to not believe them. I think heaven is a very cosy idea, because when you die you get to see all the dead people that are already there, like dead people in your family and dead people from films. Then you would have loads of people to talk to when you were waiting for all your friends and family (who are still alive) to die and meet you there. It would be like a party that never stops. I think it would be too busy, though. Another good thing about it is you could see what God's face is like. And you could ask him anything. Like, 'Why did you invent so many bad things like choking and those disgusting silverfish insects?'

Nan thinks saying 'God damn it!' and 'Jesus Christ!' is bad. I don't think she knows there are worse words you can say like 'cunt' and 'prick' and 'Fuck off, you stupid twat.' (It's OK, because I didn't say them, I only wrote them down.) 'Cunt' was Den's favourite word. My mum's was 'stop', but now she says happier words. Grandad just says 'bloody hell' all the time, especially when he is watching the news. Other things Grandad says are 'stupid bloody people', 'stupid bloody Tories' and 'I'm not bloody well'.

My grandad says the Bible is just a load of old stories. He says people wrote them to control everyone and make them get married and not moan about going to work. I don't know how stories can control people and make them do things, but Grandad is very clever, so he must be right.

Grandad doesn't believe in heaven, so I think he is going to end up in a different place to Nan when he dies. Grandad believes in science. I don't know what to believe. I keep changing my mind. I think science makes more sense than the Bible stories, because heaven sounds too good to be true, and in the Bible nobody talks about dinosaurs, and we know that they existed because of all the fossils and bones that have been found. When we know things are true they are called facts. God is not a fact, but dinosaurs are. The bad part about science is, when you die, you don't go to heaven. Instead, you just get buried in the ground, and tiny creatures eat your face off your bones, and you are just dead for ever. You don't get to see anyone you love ever again or go to a magic place in the sky. I hope heaven is real, because I never want to be away from my mum and my dad, even when we are all dead.

GOD

I have been thinking about God because of my nan. She says you can ask God for anything, but it mustn't be things like a new car or new toys. It has to be something you really need. I am asking God if he can help with my mystery. I decided to do it by letter. (Father Christmas still hasn't answered me yet.) I don't think God answers by sending a letter with the postman because Nan said, 'The lord works in mysterious ways.' I will just have to wait and see if he answers me. This is my letter:

Dear God,

Do you answer letters, or is it just prayers that people say before they go to sleep? I am writing down my prayer because I don't like saying it out loud because I feel very stupid. I hope you answer letters, because I don't know how else to get in touch.

The reason I am writing this letter is to see if you can help me with my mystery. I have tried to work out the mystery myself, but I am not getting very far. My nan says that you know everything, so I thought I would ask you.

Can you please tell me why I am made to be a girl when I am a boy? And please can you answer my best prayer and make me into a normal boy on the outside? I am already a boy, but I need some help to be a real one. Can you please help me, like the fairy helped Pinocchio? I know you are very busy with wars and with Africa, but that man Bob Geldof said he would help with that — I heard him say it on the telly. If you have got time, please think about answering my prayer. I don't mind waiting in a queue, because I know there are people with more important prayers than mine, but please hurry up if you can, because I am sick of being sad and wearing girls' knickers with itchy frills on. I've had enough, God — it's really pissing me off. My nan said you don't like swearing, but I don't think you will mind, because they are the correct words for the way I feel.

Also, I am your mistake, so I think only you can fix me. It is your job. I know you are God, but everyone makes mistakes. Other mistakes you have made are earthquakes, sadness, zoos and Dennis.

PS: I'm sorry about what those people did to your son, Jesus. Michael is right. People are just bastards.

Love from

Green (Jade) Waters

MAD

My mum went mad when I came home from school. She saw me in the yard when it was playtime, but I didn't see her. If I saw her, I would have waved and smiled. Mum didn't smile, though — she was angry because when she saw me I was only wearing half of my uniform. It was the top half. I swapped into my PE shorts and trainers in the cloakroom, and I stuffed the evil skirt into my bag. I left my long socks on and pulled them right up like football socks. They kept my legs warm. I was wearing Grandad's sun hat too, even though it's cold.

Grandad's sun hat is beige, and it's got two pockets on the sides. I keep my money in there, for the tuck shop. Mrs R always makes me take the hat off in class, though, so I just wear it in the yard. I feel nice in Grandad's hat, but my mum went mad about it because she thinks it looks silly. She said she is giving it back to him. She took my PE bag off me too. She said I can't take it every day, and she will find out which day I have got PE. Now I have to wear the evil skirt again. I am sick of it. If I was the Prime Minister, I would ban skirts for everyone, even tall girls with nice legs, like Sigourney Weaver.

DENNIS

We saw Dennis when we were walking home from the shop. I could tell it was him by his stupid monkey walk. He was on the other side of the road. He just did shark eyes, but he didn't try to speak to us – he didn't even try to speak to my sister. My mum said he lives in a flat above the bookie's now. It's OK, though, because you can't even see the bookie's from our street.

I kept checking my mum's face for tears, but there weren't any. Her eyes were just normal. I think she has used up all her tears now. I think Dennis is just like a bad nightmare that you forget when it's daytime. I hope she stays OK and Den doesn't break the law and try to come into our house again. I hope he leaves us alone for ever, because my mum is more like a normal mum now that he's gone.

PANCAKE DAY

Pancake Day is one of my favourite days. I don't know why we are not allowed to have pancakes on normal days like Mondays or Wednesdays, but when you have them it feels extra special, because you only get them once a year.

My mum made loads, and I had so many I couldn't even eat my normal tea. My mum and Verity only had one each, so there were too many left. I had loads of sugar and lemon on mine, and when I finished them I thought I was going to be sick. It was only because I was full to the brim. The brim is the top. Nan taught me that. My nan said Pancake Day is to do with Jesus. She thinks everything is to do with him. She said we have Pancake Day to use up all the eggs, and then we are not supposed to eat any because of Lent. Lent is starving yourself on purpose, even if you have got nice food in the cupboard. I think that is very stupid, and it's nasty to people who have got no food in their cupboards. The Bible makes people do very strange things.

I don't think my mum made pancakes because of the Bible. She just likes them, and she makes the best ones, because she doesn't make them too fat. She tossed them up extra high. I thought she was going to get one stuck on the ceiling. She is acting more fun now, because she has had a nice break from Dennis being horrible to her. I think she is getting much happier, because even when she does the ironing and plays her tapes she is in a different mood. She doesn't just play Tracey Chapman now, she plays the *Golden Oldies* tape – a lot. It's happier music. When she sings the songs she smiles now, instead of having a face that is like a sad, crying clown.

DOGS

When my dad was walking me home, he taught me how to kill a dog. He didn't kill a dog to teach me, he just explained how to do it. I wouldn't normally want to kill a dog, because I like them. Dogs are my favourite animal. I told my dad that I like dogs, and he laughed and said that he likes them too, but some dogs can go mad and attack you, so you have to know what to do, just in case.

My dad said that to kill a dog you have to pull their front legs apart. You have to do it really hard and quick. He said it will break their heart. I did listen, but I hope I never have to do it.

I would like a dog of my own, but my mum says we can't have one. I've got a book about dogs, though, a big yellow one called *Take Care of Your Dog*. Inside there are pictures of all the different breeds. It tells you what each breed is like. My favourite breeds are huskies and spaniels. Huskies howl like wolves and spaniels are good companions. Companions are just the dog version of friends. If I ever have a dog, I will call it Les after Les Sealey.

When I got home, I went out to play with Michael. I told him what my dad said about killing dogs. I wanted him to know because Michael is more likely to get attacked than me. There are three big dogs living in a huge kennel in his back garden.

ST DAVID'S DAY

It was St David's Day, so we had to celebrate in school. There was a special assembly, and we had to sing lots of Welsh songs. We had to dress up in old-fashioned Welsh clothes too. I asked my mum to get me a Dai cap, like Michael's, when we went shopping, but she wouldn't listen, and then when I wasn't with her she bought me all the wrong things. I cried when it was time to get dressed, because the clothes were so disgusting. At first I wouldn't put them on, but my mum said she would tell my dad, so I had to do it in the end. I looked in the mirror, and all my sadness burst out, and I was crying like mad. It was because I was so upset about the stupid clothes. The clothes I had to wear were a long itchy skirt, a white apron, a shirt with lots of frills on it, a shawl and a black scratchy hat with a ribbon. The hat was one of the worst hats I have ever put on my head. It felt very itchy and wrong. I don't think anyone should have to wear a hat that they hate. There should be a law against it.

I was mega late for school because I was still crying. When we were walking up the street, my mum started crying too, but it was the zero-noise type. I don't know why she was crying, because she didn't have to go to school in stupid granny clothes. She didn't have to wear a daffodil, either.

When I went into assembly, I felt even worse, because all the other boys were wearing leeks and nice hats and rugby shirts. Some were wearing nice waistcoats and dicky bows, too. I liked the dicky bows best, but I would have worn a rugby shirt even though I don't like rugby much. I felt very stupid in the granny hat, and it put me in an ugly brown-coloured mood.

The only good part of the day was when I went home and got changed into my tracksuit. I watched *Count Duckula* and *Inspector Gadget* with my sister, and my mum had bought us loads of Welsh cakes. I had one before tea and two after. They were lovely.

BIRTHDAY

On Wednesday it was my birthday. Now I'm eight. This birthday was much better than my last one. I was upset on my last birthday because my presents were just wrong. This time I had some really good cars. Some were Matchbox, and some were Hot Wheels. The Hot Wheels ones are the best, because they change colour when you put them in water.

The best part about my birthday was I was allowed to have the day off school. It was a special treat. My mum said she was taking me shopping for more birthday presents and some new clothes, because mine were getting too small. My mum picked the first outfit. She chose navy tracksuit bottoms, a navy and white T-shirt, a tracksuit top with a hood and special trainers which are called deck daps. I was just staring at her because my brain was trying to catch up. I couldn't believe it, because she had picked boys' stuff. Then she said I could pick any clothes I liked, as long as they were the right size. I kept pointing at things, and she kept saying, 'Yes OK. That's nice.' I was choosing things from the boys' bit of the shop, and she still said yes.

My mum found me the right sizes, and she held all the clothes over her arm. She knows how to hold lots of clothes all at once, because she used to work in a clothes shop. I picked two shirts with tiny squares on. One was blue and black, and one was red and black. I picked a grey tracksuit with a blue stripe down the side, three T-shirts, jeans and special black trousers called cords. Then I found the best-looking shirt in the world. It was dark red with a special pattern. My mum said the pattern is called paisley and the colour is called burgundy. I loved it so much I was allowed to keep it. My mum picked me loads more as well, and she even got me boys' pyjamas.

Inside the changing rooms, I asked my mum to let me keep all the new clothes, and she did. It wasn't even a trick. She even let me wear the navy tracksuit straight away. It was extra comfy. She left my old clothes in the cubicle and put the new ones in her big shopping bag. I think it's because she's not going to make me wear girly things like that again. We did our shopping very quickly, and we went straight for dinner.

When I was eating my chips I said, 'Mum, you forgot to pay.'

She said, 'Shh, eat your food.' I listened, but I kept thinking about it, and I decided that she was doing the same thing I used to do in the big shop with the Matchbox cars.

She was taking a few things because she needed them and didn't have much money. I didn't care. I was glad she did it. I don't even think God would mind if you took a couple of things if you really needed them. I normally hate shopping, but shopping for proper clothes was brilliant.

My mum finished her cup of coffee and said, 'You can wear whatever you want from now on'.

'No more skirts?'

'No more skirts.'

'What about school?'

'You can wear a tracksuit.'

It was the best thing anyone has ever said to me.

So, I don't have to wear the skirt ever again. When I found this out it made me very happy. I even jumped up and down. It was the best news I have ever had so far. My mum said I can even have black trainers, because Clarks school shoes, like the ones I normally have to wear, won't match a tracksuit. I won't even mind going to school because of it. I kissed my mum and said thanks.

She said, 'What for? I didn't do anything.'

The new clothes mean I have beaten my nemesis, like Superman when he beats Lex Luthor. It means that I am Batman, and the Joker is dead. I feel like an extra-brave warrior because I have defeated the skirt, and now I am free.

After dinner, it was the best part of the day because there was another special surprise. My mum took me to the hairdresser's, even though I'd already had a trim. The lady put a cloak around me, like Dracula's. Then she said, 'Right then, what are we doing, young lady?' When she said it, I could see my face in the mirror, and it looked like someone had coloured me in with a red felt tip. My mum told the hairdresser lady that I'm shy. Then the hairdresser asked what kind of cut I wanted, and I said, 'Please can I have a Les Sealey?' This made the lady laugh.

Then she said, 'I don't know who that is, love.'

So I said, 'OK, then, please can you cut it like Tarzan's?' This made my mum and the hair lady laugh. I don't know why people always laugh at me when I'm not telling a joke. It's extra confusing. The lady knew who Tarzan was, but she still asked my mum what kind of cut I was allowed to have. I don't know what cut my mum asked her to do, but it was the best haircut I have ever had. I was so happy, and I think my mum was happy too, because she was smiling, but at the same time tears were waiting their turn to fall out of her eyes.

My hair looks wicked now. It doesn't look like Les Sealey's, but it doesn't make me look like a girl any more. It's much shorter than it was. There was a lot of hair on the floor when the hairdresser lady had finished cutting. If I buy gel from the shop, I think I could make it look nearly the same as LS's. I don't know why my mum decided to let me do it, but I think it is because I am eight now and because she is sick of me crying and being sad. It is extra kind of her. Being eight is already better than being seven. It's brilliant.

CORTINA

Something really good happened. My mum has got a car. It is very old, but she doesn't care about that. She's just happy because she can drive, and now we don't have to wait in the rain for buses that don't turn up. The car is yellow and has got lots of patches of rust all over it. It's called a Ford Cortina, but my mum calls it 'Rust Bucket'. She loves it, though.

Dennis's dad gave the car to my mum, because he bought a new one and he doesn't need it any more. It's extra nice of him. I think he did it because he felt bad about having a nasty son. When Dennis's dad was leaving, he asked my mum if she would let him and his wife see Verity now and again. They're my sister's nan and grandad, but they are not mine, because of the different dads rule. My mum said they could see her, but she asked them never to leave Verity alone with Dennis, because she doesn't trust him to look after her properly.

The first place we went in the car was the garage. We had to go there first to get petrol. I had the window down and sat in the front seat. My sister was in the back. My mum took her shoes off to drive. She said it's easier. I don't know why it is easier, and I have never seen any other drivers take off their shoes. It must have worked, though, because we didn't crash or go through the wrong colour lights or get beeped at.

My mum is a good driver. She was extra careful because it's been ages since she passed her test, and she hasn't had any chances to drive since. She looked very happy when she was driving, and she didn't even need make-up to make her look it. It made me feel happy to spot that. Even my sister seemed happy in the back of the car, and it is always quite hard to tell if she is happy, because she doesn't say many words. I love my sister, even though we have to share a room, and her toys make it look very girly. I love Cortinas too. They are my fourth favourite car.

After we got petrol, we went to Auntie Sandra's house, because we could, even though it was Sunday. We can go anywhere we want now, and we don't have to wait to see if there is a bus. My mum and Auntie Sandra had a long chat, so me and Luke went out to play.

We played football in the long street with his friends. At first they were all saying I couldn't play with them. A boy with a giant head said, 'You can't play – you're a girl.' He said it even though I was wearing boys' clothes. Then they decided they needed another person to play five-a-side, so they let me join in. I can do more keepy-ups than the oldest boy, Justin, anyway. So I don't care what they say.

They had a real football made of leather. It was much better than the plastic ones. I scored a goal, too. It was a good game, except one boy kept tripping everyone when he couldn't get the ball, so I hurt my knee. I am used to falling on concrete, so I didn't care that much. He only tripped me because he couldn't get the ball off me in a fair way. If we were playing a real match, the referee would have given him a red card, and he would have given me a free kick. But you don't have a referee in street football – you just have cheats, cuts and tough luck. Street football is good, though. It's different to pitch football. Night-time is the best, especially if there are loads of you, and all the lampposts are working, and you can see all of the moon. Moonshine football is my best thing. It feels like everything else is still, and nothing else is happening in the world. All that exists is you and your friends and the football. Then you feel lucky to be out playing the best game in the world.

COMPLEX

My nan has given up work in the pub because she is old enough to stop working now. It is called retirement. My grandad retired ages ago, even though he was not that old. My mum said he didn't like any jobs after being in the army because he couldn't get used to not being an officer, and he couldn't get used to Civvy Street. I don't know where Civvy Street is, but I think it's where you have to go when you leave the army. It's where they send you. Anyway, my grandad didn't like it there. I don't think you are allowed to go back into the army when you leave, even if you wish you had stayed. I think it's just tough luck.

Grandad just stays at home now and watches the telly. He doesn't call it that, though – he calls it 'the box'. There are loads of names for the telly. 'Telly' is just a short word for television. Some people shorten it to TV. Grandad calls it 'the box' because it is a box with moving pictures inside. Grandad is the only person who loves films as much as me. Some people just watch them because they are on, and they are bored and have got nothing else to do, but some people really care about them.

If Grandad is not watching telly, he writes in his notebooks and reads books and listens to opera music. He only goes out if he needs something from the shop (like a newspaper or fags) or if he is visiting someone. The good news is, because Nan won't be working any more, they are going to move, to live near us. I think it is a really good idea.

My nan and grandad are going to live in a complex which is especially for older people. It is a flat, and there are lots of them all joined together. Other people's nans and grandads live there. My mum said I can still stay there, and everything will be the same. I don't think it will be at all the same, but I am glad they will be near my house. I will miss the pub, and Derek (the pool player) and the video shop.

OLD

Nan and Grandad's new flat is boiling hot, and everything is beige. I preferred the brown and orange. They brought some brown and orange furniture with them, but it's not the same.

In the complex it smells like fish and ill people. All you can hear is lots of tellies blaring. The noise is coming from all the different flats, because the old people can't hear properly, so they have their tellies turned up extra loud. If everyone is watching the same programme, you can hear the words bouncing from flat to flat down the corridor.

Nan gave Grandad a row for saying that they are trying to kill him. He said, 'Will you turn that bloody heating down. They're trying to kill us off.' I'm not sure who 'they' are, but I don't think he means the people with the loud tellies. I think he means the warden, which is the woman who is in charge of the building. The warden lives there, and it is her job to check that all the old people don't set the place on fire. It is also her job to help if anyone feels ill or is stuck or something. My nan and grandad look much younger than all the other nans and grandads. I saw one lady whose skin was nearly falling off. She looked like Skeletor. I felt sorry for her, but my nan said she was fine. She didn't look it. She looked like she had died ages ago, but her brain forgot to tell her body to stop walking around.

The new flat is much smaller than the old one, and there is only one bedroom. Mum said it is easier for Nan to clean. Grandad has only got a cupboard for his books and videos now, instead of a whole room. I am happy that they live nearer to us, though.

I think Nan likes the new place, but Grandad gets annoyed when other nans knock the door to gossip and talk rubbish. He calls them 'stupid bloody idiots'. Nan says he's rude. I don't blame Grandad, though. I don't think I would like to live in a complex either, because it is strange, and old people keep knocking the door to try to make friends with you and invite you to coffee mornings. When I am old, I would just like to be left alone to read my newspaper, so I understand Grandad. I don't think he can be bothered to make new friends at his age. It must be weird being old. Nan said it is exactly the same as being young, except with worse teeth and hair. Grandad said life goes fast, so it is important not to waste it. I think that's why he hates it when people gossip, because it is a terrible waste of time.

CORNWALL

We are going on holiday with Nan and Grandad. My mum is going to drive, and Grandad is going to pay. Nan wanted a new settee, but Grandad spent the money on the holiday instead. It is extra kind of him. I think my nan was a bit angry that she has to keep the old settee, though. I think she will realise that holidays are better than settees when she's on holiday and she's not sitting on the old settee.

Mum said that Grandad needs a break, but I don't know why. He only reads and does things he likes, so I don't know why he needs a break from that. She said the sea air will help with his headaches, too. We are going to Cornwall, which is a place in England. I haven't been to Cornwall before, and I am looking forward to going somewhere new. The people that are going are just me, Verity, my mum, Nan and Grandad. We are going for one week.

One day, when I am older, I want to go on a plane to visit somewhere far away. I have been looking in my atlas, and the place I would like to go most of all is still Canada. Canada can be very cold and it snows there a lot. There are wolves and bears there, and they also have amazing lakes. The pictures of it in my book made me want to see it in real life. I have looked at pictures of lots of countries, but I think Canada looks the prettiest. I asked my mum if we can go there one day and she laughed and said, 'We'll see.' 'We'll see' usually means no. I will go there when I am older, because nobody will be able to stop me. Going to Canada is now a plan, and it is also an ambition. When we had to do a project about a country for geography in school, I chose Canada.

ST IVES

The part of Cornwall we went to is called St Ives. We stayed in a place called a chalet, which is a bit like a caravan with no wheels that is stuck to the floor. It sounds like a normal house, but it isn't. It was strange because there was a toilet, kitchen and living room in one place, but you had to go outside to get to the bedrooms because they were in a separate building. It was the weirdest place I have ever slept. I liked it, though.

There were lots of chalets. They were spread out in two rows, and in the middle there was a giant patch of grass to play on. I played football on my own at first and then I played cricket with Grandad. I had never played it before, so I didn't know the rules. It was quite good, but not as good as football.

On the first night we went to the clubhouse, which is a kind of pub for people who are on holiday. It was wicked because I was allowed loads of pop and crisps, and they had a giant telly. When we got there, the film *Jaws* was on in one room, and in the other room there were two men singing and playing guitars. I watched the end of *Jaws* and then I listened to the singers.

My sister loved it because they played her favourite song, 'Dream'. They played loads of other songs from Mum's *Golden Oldies* tape, like 'Let It Be Me' and 'Unchained Melody'. 'Unchained Melody' is what my mum sings to us if we can't get to sleep. I liked listening to the men sing that song. They sang it quite good, but not as good as the men on the *Golden Oldies* tape. The men on the tape sing like kings. I think they sound how boy angels would sound if they are real and true and not made up.

WHISKY

We went to the beach even though it was a bit cold and you couldn't sunbathe. It was nice, though, because there weren't many other people there, so it felt like the sand and the sea was there just for us. My grandad was reading his newspaper. My sister played making sandcastles, and I helped her. My nan was just talking to my mum.

Then I played footie on my own, but the wind kept nicking the ball and trying to take it into the sea. When Grandad finished reading we played cricket. We used a hard sponge ball instead of a real cricket ball, because a real cricket ball could kill someone who is just minding their own business, enjoying a walk on the beach. I don't like to think about how I will die, because it scares me, but I wouldn't like to die by getting smashed in the head with a cricket ball. Cricket on the beach was fun, and nobody died. Grandad said it was a bonus. It was even better when everyone joined in. Grandad was extra serious about it, even though it was just beach cricket. He couldn't play for long because running made him cough like mad. I thought he was going to be sick in the sand, but he wasn't. He was just really dizzy and white.

When we'd had enough of the beach, we sat on a bench by the harbour and ate ice-cream. I had mint choc chip, because it is the best flavour. Verity had strawberry. The sea looked like it was full of floating diamonds. I told Grandad, and he said it was a good description. He smiled, but he was looking at the water in a funny way, and then he put his hand on the wall. I think he was worried he might fall off and drown in the sea. His eyes have gone extra sparkly lately. I think it is because he gets terrible headaches.

I liked looking at all the different boats. I liked their colours and their names and the way they rocked on the water but weren't going anywhere. I would be quite scared to go out to sea on a small boat, but I think I would like to sleep in a boat that was tied up nice and safe in the harbour. It would be like extra-special camping.

After the ice-cream, we went to a café because my mum wanted coffee and my grandad needed a cup of tea. Grandad always needs tea. If he doesn't have lots of cups he is like a car with no petrol. He just doesn't work. Then Nan and Grandad went back to the chalet because Grandad was ready for a sleep, but we stayed out. We had to walk around all the shops because my mum is obsessed with shopping, and whenever we go anywhere she won't go home until we have looked in every single shop. She even looks in all the rubbish ones, and she hardly ever buys anything. It takes ages and it's mega boring.

In the night-time we didn't go to the clubhouse, we stayed in the chalet, and we had fish and chips because it is Grandad's favourite. He said you have to have fish and chips when you're by the sea, but I think that is a silly rule. I didn't have fish, because I hate eating them. It makes me feel sick. Eating a fish is like eating a tiny dinosaur. I had sausage instead.

We played Scrabble when we finished our food. It's one of my favourite games. Grandad loves Scrabble, and he can spell loads of massive words that nobody has ever heard of. He always gets triple-score points. At first, everyone thinks he's making up words and cheating, but he isn't, he's just extra clever. He always has to explain the meaning of the word, and he loves it when someone gets a dictionary to check, because he already knows that he is right. He always wins, and his face dances to a song you can't hear. I wrote 'stuck', and Grandad used my U to spell out 'murder'. He won the game.

Mum and Grandad played cards after that, and I read *The Beano*. Verity just played with her doll. Mum and Nan had wine, and Grandad had whisky. Nan said he shouldn't have any, but he didn't listen. When it was time for bed, Grandad was sick from drinking too much. There was blood inside the sick. It looked like a lump of jam inside rice pudding. Mum said it was because he doesn't drink much any more. Grandad was quite angry. He said he could drink anyone under the table when he was in the army. I think he was quite different when he was in there. He was an officer, and he wore a special uniform. Now he just wears his slacks. Slacks are just normal trousers.

My dad is never sick from whisky, because he drinks it all the time and his body is used to it. My dad wouldn't be allowed in the army because he likes to make his own rules about things. In the army you have lots of rules, and everyone has to listen. You always have to be on time, so it would be no good for my dad. He is very late. Once he was a week and a half late, and he didn't even have a perfect reason. I don't think he even remembered that he had forgotten to pick me up. He didn't say anything about it, anyway.

Lots of good things happened on the holiday. It was like a picture that only had the good-coloured crayons. Everything felt nice for a change. I think it was because there was no Dennis and no skirts. I was happy because I was in comfortable clothes and my hair was right. It felt so nice. I felt like a clean, smart, Welsh soldier.

MY FAVOURITE PARTS OF THE HOLIDAY:

- Going to the beach.
- Having a BBQ on the green.
- Playing football.
- Eating ice-cream every day.
- Scrabble.
- Hearing my mum laugh and talk when I was half asleep.
- Sleeping in the same room as my mum and my sister.
- Swimming in the indoor swimming pool.

I didn't swim in the sea because it was too cold. I was also too scared of drowning. I wanted to buy a dinghy and have a go in the sea, but I didn't feel brave enough to chance it. Dinghies are just tiny little blow-up boats. I would rather have a little boat in the pool. It's safer than the sea. The sea is dangerous because of the tide. You could be having a good time and forget that you are floating out. You could also be eaten by a shark. I saw it happen to people in the film *Jaws*. They were having a lovely time, and then they were screaming and then they were dead.

FA CUP

I watched the football with Grandad because it was the FA Cup Final. The teams playing were Manchester United and Crystal Palace. It was an exciting game, and it went on for ages. There were loads of goals. At the end, it was 3–3. Grandad said it means they have to have a rematch on another day. You are not allowed to draw in an FA Cup Final because someone has to win to get the cup. If you draw, you just have to play again. It is a strange rule. I liked the Manchester United team, and I liked their shirts. I wish I had one.

REPLAY

I was allowed to watch *Match of the Day* at home (even though my mum doesn't like football) because it was a special match. It was the FA Cup Final replay. I was extra excited when the music came on. There were loads of balloons everywhere, and before the game started there were soldiers in red coats on the pitch playing trumpets, and everybody was singing the national anthem. It was the English anthem 'God Save the Queen', because the match was in Wembley, and that is in England. Also, the teams were English, and there were English royal people there like the Duke of Kent. I only know about the royal people because I always listen to everything Des Lynam says.

After the singing, the players came on to the pitch. I couldn't believe it when Des Lynam told me that Les Sealey was playing for Manchester United. He said he is on loan from Luton Town. I think it means they are borrowing him to see if they like him. My eyes wouldn't believe it when I saw him. I think I miss lots of football news because my mum doesn't always let me watch football programmes. She hardly ever watches telly, anyway. She didn't even look when the game was on. She just did the polishing and she made me a little picnic – it was cheese and crackers, crisps and a pint of squash.

Both the teams were wearing different colours to the last time they played. I think their shirts from Saturday are still dirty. This time Man United wore red shirts, and Crystal Palace wore black and yellow stripes. They looked like bees.

Even though I haven't picked my favourite team, I had to support Man United when I found out about Les playing for them. It was extra exciting when they scored. The goal happened like this: McClair – Wallace – Webb – Martin – GOAL! It was wicked. Palace didn't score any goals because Les Sealey is the best. I lost count of how many saves he made, but I think it was about three. He saved a free kick with his leg, and he was very good at getting his legs in the way of shots. He looked like a giant spider wearing a green jumper. I think Man United will want to keep him for ever now. I was glad they won, but I felt a bit sorry for Crystal Palace, because it must be hard to lose in a cup final. It must be hard lines for the whole team.

CHURCH

Me and Luke went to church with Nan. I've been to church before, but Nan's new church was strange and confusing. We listened to the church man (the pastor), and at first, he was just doing normal prayers, but then he started talking rubbish — he wasn't even saying real words. It was quite scary, because it was a shock at first, and I couldn't tell what my nan was thinking, because her eyes were closed.

When the pastor spoke, some of the other people started speaking back to him in funny language. I think it's called gobbledygook. Me and Luke were trying not to laugh, but we couldn't help it, because it was the funniest thing ever. It felt like everyone had gone mad. It was like they were all shouting at each other, but nobody knew what anyone else was saying. They all sounded like Klingons from the programme *Star Trek*.

It is very hard not to laugh at people when they are all talking bollocks nonsense. I stuffed my jumper inside my mouth so I wouldn't make a noise, but water started leaking from my eyes. It was my laugh escaping. Then a woman stood up and shouted, 'Praise the lord, cover us with the blood of Jesus!' And then it happened: Luke couldn't help it. His laugh just burst out. It was really loud. You could hear it all around the church, and then mine fell out too, and when it started, I couldn't stop it.

You are not supposed to laugh in church because it is rude. Church is not even meant to be funny, but it is one of the funniest things I have ever seen. Nan was a bit annoyed about us laughing, but she didn't get too cross. I think she could understand why we couldn't help it. We didn't have a row, anyway. I think she found it half funny too, even though she's a Christian. On the way home, she explained that the made-up language is called Tongues. She said it's a special language that only God knows. I still think it's called Nonsense, and I wish she had warned us about it before we went, but grown-ups always forget to tell you important things. It's just the rules.

Mrs R taught us about God in class. We learnt about Jesus and his disciples and about Adam and Eve. She said Adam and Eve were the first people on Earth. She said Earth was nice – there were no spiders, snakes, wars or earthquakes – but then everything went wrong. It happened because Eve didn't listen to God, and she ate an apple that she wasn't supposed to eat. It made God very angry, so he banished Adam and Eve and made lots of bad things to punish them. 'Banished' is just a big word for 'sent away'. I asked Mrs R why the apple was there if Eve wasn't allowed to eat it. I think that is very stupid. It is like God having a party (with nice cakes and sandwiches) and telling you not to eat anything. Mrs R didn't really answer. She hates it when you ask questions, even if you put your hand up first.

I read about Adam and Eve and the beginning of the world in the Children's Bible, but I thought the story was very stupid because there were no dinosaurs in it, and everybody knows dinosaurs were on Earth before people. So, I think someone just made it up. Mrs R said that made-up stories are called fiction, and true stories are called non-fiction. They are also called factual. I think the Bible might be fiction, but I am still trying to work out what to think about God, because I am not sure yet – I can't decide. I think I am like Grandad, and I believe in science, but I haven't told anyone, especially my nan, because religious people can get upset if you don't believe in the same things as them. Science people do not mind. They don't get upset about silly things.

Also, I don't understand why God lets bad things happen if he can fix them. For example, there are lots of people who haven't got any money or food, and God could fix it, but he doesn't. It is a mystery.

OTHER THINGS I DON'T UNDERSTAND ABOUT GOD:

1. How did he create Earth in six days? It takes ages just to build one house or dig up one road. God is much quicker than the council men.
2. Why didn't he do anything on the Sunday? It is a bit lazy.
3. Why does he let people starve?
4. How is he the same person as Jesus? My nan said God is Jesus, but she also said Jesus is God's son. I think she is confused because she is getting old.
5. Where is he?

6.   Where is heaven? My nan said it's up in the sky, past the clouds, but that can't be true, because if you go up higher than the clouds you end up in space. If heaven was in space, I think astronauts would have found it, or someone would have spotted it with a telescope.

7.   If God didn't make dinosaurs, he couldn't have made Earth, because dinosaurs were here once. There is proof in the museum we went to on our school trip.

8.   Who made God?

9.   What about the Big Bang? My grandad told me about the Big Bang. He said there was a giant explosion in space, and after that tiny things started to join together and come to life. It took ages to join enough bits together to make a dog or a horse, though. Grandad said that at first there were little animals that were very small, and then after a long time there were humans. It's hard to understand, but it still makes more sense than the Bible.

10. Why didn't he answer my letter? Why did he make me wrong on the outside? Why did he give me an ugly, disgusting vagina? It is not fair.

CANCER

Grandad is ill. It is not the kind of illness that can be fixed with medicine, so now he will die. It is disgusting news. It is also a shock. I asked my mum when he will die, but she got upset and said that she couldn't put an exact time on it, because, 'Not everything is set in fucking stone'. I am upset about Grandad, but I am also upset for my mum and my nan.

The type of illness Grandad has got is called lung cancer. It means his lungs are not working properly. They have been destroyed and gone black like a burnt-out car. Nan said it's because he is a chain smoker. When they went to see the doctor, the doctor told Grandad he has got six weeks to live. Grandad said, 'I told you I was bloody ill.' He also said there's no point giving up now, and he has been smoking even more fags than usual. Now it makes sense that Grandad has to go and have a lie down in the middle of the day. It's because cancer makes you tired. And it might be why he gets terrible headaches.

I don't want Grandad to die, but I haven't said anything about it to anyone. Grandad is one of my favourite people ever. I don't think he knows that, though, because I have never told him. It must be horrible if a doctor tells you you've only got six weeks to live. The school summer holiday is six weeks, and that goes really quickly. If I was running out of time and life, I would borrow the money and go to Canada. I wish I could take Grandad to Canada before he dies. I bet he would like to see it, and it would be nice to see it together. We could go on a boat trip on a turquoise lake that is very beautiful and perfect. I am sad that we can't do it, but I haven't told anyone that either. I drew a picture of me and Grandad on a lake in Canada, but I didn't show anyone. I just put it under my pillow to turn it into a dream.

FISH AND CHIPS

Today Grandad wanted fish and chips again. They had to be from a certain chip shop, which is on an estate where I used to live when I was a baby. He said they make the best chips around. My mum went to get them, and I went with her. I didn't have fish, though, because I still don't like it, even when they are disguised with batter and you can't see the scales, because you still know they are just regular fish underneath. I had a pie this time. Grandad was right about the chips. They were lovely. The estate was disgusting, though. There was junk everywhere and smashed windows. I'm glad we don't live there any more.

It was weird to have dinner with Grandad and be thinking about the cancer and the dying at the same time. It was strange because he seemed OK, even though he will be dead in six weeks. I think Grandad just wanted to eat nice food while he's still got the chance. It is hard to describe what it was like at Nan and Grandad's, because we didn't really have a nice time because everyone was sad, but it was sort of nice if you tried not to remember about the cancer. It felt the way it looks when somebody scribbles over red with blue on a picture.

SELFISH

Grandad is much worse now. I heard my mum talking about it to Auntie Sandra. She said you can see the cancer on his skin and in his eyes. She didn't say what colour it was, but I think cancer's colour is yellow. My mum has been staying at my nan and grandad's in the daytime because she is helping to look after him. It is very hard for her, because she has to look after us as well. Someone else has to look after him in the night. They have to take it in turns, because my nan can't do it all on her own. Auntie Sandra and Auntie Carol are helping. Auntie Carol is staying in Wales and can't go home to England.

Most of the time my mum is just tired and sad. I am sad except when I am playing football, and then I feel like nothing can go wrong and nothing can hurt me, as long as I keep going. I felt bad today because my mum asked me if I wanted to go and see Grandad, and I said no, because I was playing footie with Michael and his brother. I sort of wanted to go, but I sort of didn't want to see Grandad now that he can't get out of bed and you can see the cancer on him. I am scared to see it. I just kept playing football. But when I went home I felt selfish and sad. I have been thinking a lot about Grandad, but I haven't been to see him since the fish and chips day. When I saw him last, the cancer was still hiding.

GONE

My mum was crying in a very strange way, and I had to cwtch her because she was going mad. She just kept saying, 'My dad's dead, my dad's gone,' over and over. I wished someone was there to help, because it is quite scary when mums cry in a mad way. I didn't cry, because I couldn't concentrate on my sadness because my mum's sadness stopped her legs working properly. I had to help her to get up off the stairs and go and sit down on the settee. I didn't know what to say, because it is hard to find anything good to say when somebody is dead.

It was quite hard to imagine Grandad as a dead person, because he was eating fish and chips the last time I saw him, and I don't think he was ready to die. He was only 62. It's not that old. Some people live to be 100. It's not fair.

I didn't let any sadness out until I was in my room in bed. Then I thought about all the times my mum had asked me to go and see him, and I didn't go because I was nervous and scared and I just wanted to play football instead. I wished I had gone, because I never said goodbye. That is called regret. I know because every time I didn't understand a word when we played Scrabble, Grandad read me the word and the meaning from the dictionary. Regret can score you lots of points in Scrabble, but it feels really bad when it happens to you in real life.

WRONG

I did some workings out, and I found out that the doctor who said Grandad had six weeks to live got his sums wrong. Grandad died after seven weeks, not six. I think he got an extra week because he was kind and good and always made everything feel nice and warm. I didn't say this to anybody, because sometimes when I say things and ask too many questions at bad times people get annoyed. Also, I didn't want to say the wrong things to my mum, because she is extra sad. I know because she was drinking wine, and she doesn't normally drink it on her own — she only drinks when there is a party. She was smoking, too, and she doesn't even smoke any more. She gave up ages ago.

I hope my mum doesn't get lung cancer. I am already too sad about Grandad. Even though I knew he was going to die because cancer gives you a warning, it was still hard to believe it when it happened. Seven weeks isn't enough time to get used to somebody you love dying. I don't think your heart and brain can ever get used to it. I was very sad. I only cried when I was in bed, though, and I did zero-noise crying, so nobody heard me.

ZOMBIE

My mum's sadness has stayed for ages this time. It's like a visitor who is a nuisance. I used to think her sadness could be fixed for ever as long as she had a nice boyfriend, but I have worked out that people can turn sad for lots of reasons. Sometimes people can even get sad when there's nothing to be sad about. This time I think my mum is still sad because of Grandad. I think that's what turned her into a zombie again. I don't think mums go zombie on purpose. I think they just turn zombie when they are sad and tired all at once.

I'm trying to help by being extra good, and I don't moan about anything, even if it's fish fingers for tea. Nan is helping too. I don't think mum will go full zombie this time, because she hasn't got anyone being nasty to her now. She sort of comes back to normal when she has to tell us to do something or when she makes dinner. She just does it all in zombie style with marble eyes. Then she goes back to bed. It's a good job Nan can come over all the time. She wouldn't be able to if Grandad was still here. She would be running around like a mad chicken.

I don't know what fixes zombied mums. I think it's a mixture of sleep, food and kindness. I hope she doesn't stay like it for ever. I don't know what to do about it. She is acting the way she acted when those girls stole my bike.

She just cries and looks at the wall. It is too sad. I am glad my nan is here to help, but I wish Grandad was here too. He always made things feel nicer, just by talking in his lovely voice. I wish I had his voice on tape, because I don't want to forget what it sounded like. It's hard to remember voices, even voices that you love.

MAGIC

My dad looked after me for two nights this week because my mum has got a lot to sort out, and I haven't been to his house for ages, so it's just fair. It was nice to have a break from worrying all the time, even though I did still think about my mum and Grandad and everything. I wasn't really in the mood to go out and play football for once, and Aaron was sulking because he wanted to go. In the end, I went, just to get the stupid sad spud look off his face. I was glad I did, though, because we went to the park so we could play properly.

We did one-twos all the way up the pitch, and we took shots at the proper-sized goals, even though there was no goalkeeper. It didn't matter, because it was just for practice. I practised penalties, and the feeling of the ball moving off my foot and curving in the air made me feel like a bird that could fly, even though I was still standing on the ground. I watched the ball go into the top corner of the goal, and it made me feel magic. All the sounds and ideas and whizzing went out of my head, and it was just quiet and still, and all I cared about was the look and the shape of the ball going into the right place. That is why I love football. It is like magic medicine. It can save you from being sad. It can even save you from the world.

FUNERAL

It was my grandad's funeral, and I wasn't allowed to go. I even had to go to school and act like it was just a normal day. I went mad, and I even swore. It was the worst row I have EVER had with my mum. She wouldn't listen to me, and she just kept saying, 'You're not going, you're too young.' That doesn't even make sense. It is also incorrect, because anyone is allowed to go to a funeral. It doesn't matter how old you are. I was really angry, but I tried to swallow the feeling because of my mum. She was staring out of the window in the kitchen and doing zero-noise crying. I was in an ugly brown-crayon mood, though. I really wanted to go to Grandad's funeral so I could say goodbye. You should be allowed to go to a funeral if you loved the dead person. Nobody should be allowed to stop you, not even your mum.

My mum and my aunties looked quite strange in their funeral clothes. They looked very smart at the same time, though. Auntie Carol was wearing a black vale and lace gloves, and my mum was wearing a hat that belonged to someone in a zero-colour film. Auntie Sandra was the only one who looked normal and comfortable, because she just had an ordinary black blouse and black trousers on. If I was allowed to go, I would have asked my mum to buy me a plain black tracksuit and plain black trainers. One of the good things about Grandad was he didn't care about rubbish things. He never cared about people's clothes, and he never ever said I couldn't wear boys' clothes. I think it was because he was always interested in talking about other things that are much more important, like the 'stupid bloody Government'.

I don't know everything that happened at the funeral because I wasn't there. I just know they played Grandad's favourite opera music. Grandad's best opera song was a song by two men who sing about loving the same girl. I know it because I've heard it lots of times. His other favourite was sung by a girl with an extra-high voice. Her song is about having a row with her dad because he won't let her marry the boy she loves. It is funny to have row songs at your funeral. The songs are not sung in English, but I know what the people are singing about, because Grandad always used to tell me. He used to translate the words into English when they were singing. I know the songs off by heart because Grandad played them over and over again in the big flat. Even though I wasn't listening to the songs properly, because I was reading or playing, they just sort of jumped into my brain. I think that means they are very good songs, because even if you try to ignore them, they make you take notice.

They didn't have a priest or a vicar at the funeral. Instead, an ordinary lady did the speaking. She said nice things about Grandad. Auntie Carol also read something, and then, when everybody went home, they burnt Grandad in a big oven until he broke into ashes.

When I think of Grandad burning in an oven it makes me think of toast, because my mum always burns it. Sometimes it goes completely black, and when you bite it, it just crumbles and turns to soot. I think Grandad wanted to be cremated like toast because he was a bit worried about being buried. When you are buried, maggots eat your eyeballs and your skin. I don't think that part worried Grandad, though. I think he was scared because of the film we watched where a man was buried alive. It happened because people thought he was dead. He was screaming and scratching at the box, trying to get out, and then he died because there wasn't enough air, and he didn't have any water or food. It was a horrible way to die. There is no chance of waking up alive if you get burnt into ashes. I don't like the sound of being burnt or buried. I think they are both rubbish choices. I think they should invent something new. I hope they do when it's my turn to be dead.

CEMETERY

I went to the cemetery to see where they put Grandad's ashes. He wasn't buried because of the burning. They just buried his ashes in the ground. You can't tell who got burnt and who got eaten by maggots when you look at the graves. They all look the same. It was weird looking at Grandad's spot, because it didn't feel like he was under the dirt.

The cemetery was nice, though. It had lots of birds and flowers. Nan was doing zero-noise crying. People always cry when they look at graves, but I don't know why, because graves are just like cupboards for bones and ashes. I don't think dead people are really in graves. I think they are in memories and photographs and living inside people's hearts. When you die, your energy is over. That's science, not religion. I didn't say that to Nan, though, because she thinks Grandad is waiting for her in heaven. I hope he is. It's a nice idea. I felt sorry for her, so I helped her to plant the flowers and keep the grave tidy.

Grandad's spot is in between two women. Nan said that it would make him happy, and she did a strange little laugh, even though her eyes were still full of tears. One lady was called Edith Jones, who died when she was 64, and the other one was called Alice Roberts, who didn't have a long turn at living. It must be strange to be buried next to people you don't know. If I ever get buried, I want to be on my own with nobody next to me, and I want my grave to say GREEN, *not* JADE.

SECRET BOOK CLUB

Since Grandad died, I have been going into his cupboard a lot. I sit in there because it is extra cosy, and it smells of him. Sometimes I wear his hat, too. Then I look at all the videos and books, and I read the video-index book. That's my favourite. It tells you what films are in the cupboard and which actors are in the films. For example, video number 73 is *Who's Afraid of Virginia Woolf?* The actors in it are called Richard Burton and Elizabeth Taylor. Richard Burton was Grandad's favourite. He even talked like him. Richard Burton was Welsh, and he had a voice like that lovely rain that feels like it's kissing you. Elizabeth Taylor is extra beautiful, and she's got the loveliest eyes I've ever seen. Grandad told me they are a special sort of blue that sometimes looks violet. Violet is an unusual colour – not many people have that inside their eyeballs. You can't see the colour of her eyes on the telly, because the films are in black and white. She still looks beautiful, though. I think you must be extra beautiful if you can shine when the telly takes all the colours out of you.

My nan doesn't understand why I like being in the cupboard. She always says, 'Come on, come out of there, you'll get covered in dust,' but I don't listen. Last time I was there, I stayed in the cupboard for ages. I was just reading Grandad's writing. I followed his words with my fingers. It felt like I could touch him.

Nobody knows, but I have decided to be in a special, secret book club with Grandad. I am going to read all the books in his cupboard. I'm going to watch all his films, too. Then it will be like he is still talking to me and telling me interesting things. I think it will be extra hard, though, because most of his books are big, and even some of the titles are hard to read. I am going to do it, though, because I want to be as clever as Grandad one day. It's my best plan.

MONGREL

My dad picked me up, and I was really happy because I missed him loads. It felt like I hadn't seen him for ages. He's got a new dog called Tiggy. Aaron picked the name. If I had a dog, I would still call it Les, after Les Sealey. Tiggy is a girl dog, which is called a bitch. Sometimes people call other people bitches as a way of being nasty. I don't know why it's nasty, though.

Tiggy is brown and black, and she's a mongrel. A mongrel is a type of dog that is mixed from different breeds. I am a mongrel person, because my outside and inside self is mixed up. I like dogs because they don't care if you are a boy or a girl. They only care if you are kind and feed them and don't tie them up and leave them out in the rain. Tiggy is not a puppy. She is a full-sized dog. My dad got her because his friend was getting rid of her. She is allowed out at any time on her own. All she has to do is scratch the door. I told my dad he is supposed to walk the dog and not let her walk herself, but he just laughed and said, 'She'll be all right, nobody will steal her, and if they did, they'd bring her straight back.'

Tiggy doesn't look like the kind of dog that would get stolen. She doesn't look like the kind of dog that might go crazy and try to kill you either. She has got dopey eyes, and she's not that fast. She's the kind of dog who is not a danger. She's the kind of dog that you could be friends with.

SIMPLE SIMON

This man was sitting on the wall and telling everyone jokes. He said his name was Simple Simon. I think he was called simple because he was acting very strange, or he might have just been drunk, because he was drinking a can. He was being very stupid, but it was also a bit funny to watch. Some kids were asking him lots of questions – they were trying to find out all about him because nobody had seen him before. He just kept saying his name was Simple Simon. I think it's a nickname, because nobody would call their own kid that. I didn't ask anything. I was just with Michael, and we were just listening. The man was telling people to do things by doing the rhyme game Simple Simon Says. He started making strange noises and barking like a dog, too. Then he was acting like a chicken, clucking and pretending he had wings. Ricky came out and went mad. He said, 'Oi! What you doing? Get the fuck away from here now. If I see you around here again I'll give you a fucking hiding.'

Simple Simon got off the wall and mumbled something. He walked up the road and started shouting, but I don't know what he was saying because he wasn't speaking properly.

I had a massive row when my mum found out. It is because Simple Simon is a stranger, and my mum said he could have been a nutter. I think he was a nutter, because he wasn't making much sense, and you don't normally see adults going around acting like animals. I don't think he was trying to be nasty or do anything wrong, though. But I promised not to do it again. If I see him again, I have to tell my mum straight away. My mum is only strict about some things. For example, she is strict about strangers, but she doesn't care if we are ten minutes late for school. Michael's mum and dad are not strict about anything, apart from letting your dinner go cold. We had beans on toast for tea, because we didn't have any other food left in the cupboard.

STREET

Today I played in the street until 8 o'clock. I was allowed because it is nearly summertime, and that means it stays lighter in the night-time for longer. My mum was in the mood to let me, anyway. Michael let me have a turn on his bike, but I fell off because the chain kept coming off, and

I wasn't used to it. When I fell, I landed on the handlebar, and it got stuck in my stomach. I cried, but I didn't do loud crying. My mum made me go inside for a bath, even though loads of kids were still out playing. It wasn't even dark, but my mum said that makes no difference because it doesn't get dark till late. So it was still bedtime, even though the sky had been coloured in by a nice, pale-blue crayon.

Michael was allowed to stay out very late. He was still out after I had my bath, when I was lying in bed, reading my book. My reading book is called *George's Marvellous Medicine* by Roald Dahl. It's extra funny, but I couldn't concentrate on reading, because everyone was still out and I could hear them playing. I kept getting up to look through my bedroom window. I could see Michael. He is lucky that he can stay out late, but he is unlucky in other ways. He is unlucky to have black teeth, and he is unlucky to have clothes that are too small. My clothes used to be for girls, but they were never the wrong size.

SLEEPOVER

My mum was in quite a good mood, so I asked if Michael could sleep over, and she said 'OK' in the end because I was nagging. She won't always let him, because sometimes he wets the bed. It's not his fault, though. It's just by accident.

When we went in, we watched a film that Auntie Sandra lent us. It was called *Back to the Future*. It was about a boy called Marty McFly, who goes back in time in a time machine that his friend invented. It is a wicked film. I have asked my mum to buy me it on video so I can see it again.

We had to sleep top and tail, but I didn't mind. I was at the top because it's my bed. It's hard to fall asleep when you've got someone to talk to, though. Me and Michael were awake for ages. We talked about the film, and he told me about the films he watched over his uncle Gary's. He's got millions. I told him about Grandad's films that he nicked off the telly. I don't remember falling asleep, because we were having too much fun. Michael didn't even piss on me in the night. When you're happy, it's hard to remember the picture of what you were doing and everything that happened. It all just goes into a nice blur. If the day was a colour, it would have been bright orange.

TIME MACHINE

I am still trying to work out some things about being a boy. I know I definitely am a boy, but I'm still angry that I have been made into a girl on the outside. It's making me really upset, because I don't understand it. Sometimes I try to forget about it and get away from the problem, but it's impossible because you can't run away from yourself, you're always stuck with you.

I've got to work out what happened to me, though. It's hard because nobody listens to me, and nobody understands. I don't want to ask my mum about it any more, because I hate it when she looks sad, and I don't think I should ask my dad after he got annoyed about the Indian lie. I wish I asked Grandad, because I think he might have known the answer, because he was so clever, but I couldn't ask him, because I was too shy and embarrassed. I definitely can't ask my nan. She will just think I am being naughty. So I am still stuck, and it is still a mystery.

I think I am just a normal boy inside and a disabled boy on the outside. We always have to learn about disabled people in school because it is a school that disabled people can go to if they like. It is because it's not fair to send them to a special school. When we do lessons about being disabled, it sounds like me and the way I feel. It is invisible to everyone else, though.

If I had a time machine, like Marty McFly, I would go back to before I was born and fix the things that went wrong and made me like this. In the 'choose your own adventure' book from the library, if things go wrong, you can just go back to the beginning and have a new adventure. You can just try again until you get things right. You get another chance. You can go back and choose the right option, so you don't get caught in a storm or die in a plane crash or have a girl's body when you're a boy.

SCRAP

I've got a new bike. It isn't really new, it's second hand, but I don't care about that. Somebody chucked it out. My dad found it up the scrap yard. The scrap yard is where metal things go if they are broken or nobody wants them. I can't believe someone took my bike there. They must have been rich. There's nothing even wrong with it – everything works, even the brakes.

I felt extra lucky when my dad gave it to me. It was a big surprise, because he just turned up and he was pushing it down the street. It's not even my birthday or Christmas. It's just a present for nothing, for free.

My new bike is white, and it's got blue tyres and a blue seat. It says Skyway on the bar, next to some little red stripes. It's wicked. I couldn't wait to show Michael. I even left my dad in my house because I was so excited. Michael didn't even ask to have a go, but I let him anyway, because he always lets me have a go on his bike when I'm fed up of walking. We went straight up the park, and it was nice that we didn't have to take turns. We went on the longest ride. Even when the sun sank under the mountain I didn't want to go home. I just wanted us to keep going for ever.

FLYING

Today I rode my bike with no hands. I could already do it one-handed, but I have been practising riding with none. It was mega hard at first, and trying to do it took up all of the day. Michael was showing me all the time, and I kept copying, but at first I had to keep grabbing the handlebar with one hand. We had to find a perfect flat place to do it, and that was hard, because there are so many hills.

We went into the pub car park to practise. It's up on the main road. I decided not to go home until I could do it. We kept going round and round in giant circles, and then it happened. I got my balance and my bravery at the same time and let go. It was the best feeling. It was like flying, but different. It was like cycling through the sky on a bike that floated along with you. When I did it I thought about birds, and I think I found out exactly what they feel like when they fly. Birds don't ride bikes, so it sounds funny, but riding my bike with no hands was my version of being a bird. I don't think I can ever get nearer to being a real one. Not even if I grew wings and feathers.

STRANGERS

Because it was the last day of school we were allowed to play in the morning, and in the afternoon we all had to go into the hall to watch a film. I thought it was going to be a normal film, but it was another warning film. It was called *Say No to Strangers*. It wasn't a very fun film, because it was about learning not to get taken by someone who wants to do bad things to you.

The film explained that you can't tell if a person is nice or nasty by looking at them. It showed the main things you mustn't do as well. You must never go into lonely places on your own, and you must never go anywhere with a stranger. You should always tell your mum or dad where you are going. And I almost forgot: if you think someone is suspicious you must tell your mum, dad, a teacher or a policeman. If you stick to all the rules, you probably won't get nicked.

After the warnings, the film showed a girl called Theresa getting into a car with a stranger outside her school at home time. She did it because he said he would give her a lift and her mum knew about it, but he was lying. He also gave her sweets. Sweets are strangers' favourite trick. It's how they get you to go with them. Theresa went with the man because he said he would give her a lift home, and it would be OK, but it wasn't OK. Really, he took her to his house, and he tried to kiss her and make her take her clothes off. Theresa was lucky because she shouted for help and escaped. She could have got sexed and killed, though. The invisible man on the telly said, 'Take care – you don't want to end up dead or in hospital. Say NO to strangers.'

I know all about strangers because of my mum and dad. I still listened, though, because I never want to get taken. We've seen loads of warning films at school. It makes you scared of everything. I saw one about fire and one about electricity, but the worst one was *Lonely Water*. It was about a devil trying to drown kids if they went swimming in dangerous places like a marsh or a lake. It was extra scary. It made me extra careful about the black bog, though. I never go too close to it. If we go over there, I always get scared I will fall in, so most of the time I stay up on the wall.

After the film, we were all allowed to take our books home. We will have new ones next year because we are going into a new class. Mr W is going to be our new teacher, but first we have got six weeks to play football and have a nice time.

BORING

I went to call for Michael, but he wasn't there. His mum said he was already out somewhere, but I couldn't find him. I looked everywhere, even down by the river and over the black bog, but I gave up looking in the end.

It was quite boring in the street, because there was nobody to play with. I kicked the ball against the wall and did keepy-ups, but then I went back in because I was fed up.

It was boring in the house, too. My mum was cleaning, because she's only half zombie now. It means she is sometimes normal. My sister was watching telly, so I went upstairs and started writing. I'm practising my writing because there is no school for ages, and even though it's nice to have a holiday and not get up early, sometimes you miss writing and books and the comfy feeling of learning new things. So I wrote a story. It was about a boy who went back in time and lived with an Indian tribe. The Indians thought the boy was strange because he wasn't at all like them, but they were kind to him and looked after him. The boy helped the Indians too, and together they stopped the cowboys taking their land. It's an adventure story. I tried to make it interesting, but writing good stories is hard work. You have to work extra hard, even if you have got a good imagination and you're in top group.

When I finished the story I went downstairs and watched telly with my sister, even though it was a boring programme. I decided to give up in the end because it was a just a boring day. Not every day can be a good one. Sometimes you just get fed up. You can even get fed up with the things you like. Sometimes even your favourite things get on your fucking nerves.

HUNTING

Michael called for me and asked if I wanted to go hunting with him and his uncle Gary. My mum said I could go, even though she hates guns and people killing things. She thinks you should only kill something if you are going to eat it – not just for nothing, not just for fun. She still let me go, though.

We went hunting down by the rope-swing tree. On the tree there is a metal warning sign. Somebody wrote the warning with white paint. It says, 'PRIVATE FISHING – ANYONE CAUGHT FISHING WITHOUT A LICENSE OR A DAY TICKET WILL BE PROSECUTED.' I bet the person who wrote it loves fish and is sick of people nicking them out of the river.

Gary didn't bring his fishing rod. He just brought his gun. He said we could have a go if we wanted. Michael had a turn first. When it was my go I was a bit scared. The gun was extra heavy, and it was hard to aim and shoot. Gary had to help me. I shot it once and gave it back. I didn't kill anything, luckily. I was glad. My shot just went in the air.

Me and Michael sat down and watched when Gary was trying to shoot birds. I kept hoping he would miss. He missed loads. Then he got one. It made a horrible noise when it fell out of the tree and landed on the riverbank. It was completely still like a stone.

Its feathers moved, but that was just because of the wind. It made me feel very sad. Michael was sad about the dead bird too. We just stood there looking at it. It was hard to think it was dead, even though we knew it was. You kept expecting it to just get up and fly away. I think Michael was too scared to say anything because he went extra quiet.

Gary scooped the bird up in his hand. He kissed it and said, 'Hello fatty.' He was laughing too. Then he said he was going to put the bird into a pie and eat it. I didn't believe him, though. I've never heard of it, anyway. I think it's a lie. It must be. Nobody would want to eat a bird pie. It's a ridiculous idea.

I've decided going hunting was a mistake, and I'm never going again. I can't stop thinking about the poor bird. It was just minding its own business, sitting in a tree, and then it was dead. It is very sad to die, especially if it was for nothing, and especially if you end up in a disgusting pie.

CWTCH

Michael was sat on the curb when I found him. He was crying, and his tears had made two grey lines down his face, like train tracks. I asked him what was wrong, but he wouldn't tell me. He just said, 'Nothing.' I don't know what happened. He hardly ever cries. I've only seen him cry if he has a very bad fall and when he has a row off his dad. I didn't know what to do, so I sat on the curb next to him to keep him company. That's what you do when you're best friends. You stick together, even when everything is rubbish. I put my arm around Michael because his tears wouldn't stop.

It's not nice to see someone feeling sad, especially if they're lovely and you can't figure out a way to help them, but sometimes you just have to let someone be sad, without knowing the reason. Sometimes all you can do is give them a cwtch. A cwtch says all the kind words without you speaking anyway.

LIGHT

When I woke up, I thought my mum would be in bed, but she wasn't, she was up, and she was acting normal again. Her eyes even had normal lights back in them. She was talking and painting and seemed extra busy. I think it is because she has been sleeping so much and has saved up her energy, and now it's bursting out of her. It was very hard to get used to her new mood, but I was glad she was feeling better. She made us eggs and dippers, and she ate all hers. It felt like everything was going halfway back to normal. The mood in the house wasn't the dark-crayons mood for a change. It was more like turquoise.

READING

My mum's new hobby is reading. She used to read a bit, but now she does it all the time. I think reading is a very good hobby, because it means you are enjoying yourself and getting cleverer at the same time. It is nice to see my mum doing it. She keeps going to the library and getting new books. I am reading a book called *Huckleberry Finn*. I found it in Grandad's cupboard. It's extra hard to understand because the narrator talks funny. The narrator is the person who is telling the story. It is good, though. It's about a boy called Huckleberry, who is on a big adventure. Huckleberry Finn reminds me of Michael. They both hate wearing shoes and having a bath and being told what time to go home.

I am reading a lot because school doesn't start for ages, so I have to learn things by myself. I'm also reading a lot because I want to be extra clever like Grandad was. I am still in the secret book club, but it's not really a secret any more. Even though the books are too hard for my age, I am enjoying trying to read them. Nan wanted to give them to the pastor to sell in the church sale, but I wouldn't let her.

It's lovely and cosy when everyone reads, especially if the big lamp is on. It is extra quiet, but in a nice way. Even my sister joins in and reads her baby books. It's brilliant, because we're all together in the same room, but we are also in different places because our books send us on different adventures. Reading a book feels like you are travelling through space, and you can see what another world is like, but you can still come home in time for dinner without being in danger. If you don't read books, you are just stuck in one world and you are missing out on millions of others.

GARAGE

When we went to the garage for petrol, the man who works there gave my mum a piece of paper with her change. It said 'Ring Me' and it had a phone number. I didn't see him do it, because I was waiting in the car with Verity. My mum was smiling when she came out, so I think she was happy about it. I don't really know why the garage man asked her to ring him. He doesn't even know her. I think he probably fancies her. That's the only reason you would give a lady your number. When I am older, I am going to give my phone number to Sigourney Weaver. I will give it to Elizabeth Taylor, too, if she is still alive. I think my mum would be happier if she had a nice boyfriend, so I think she should ring the number and go out with the garage man. She has been lonely for ages now.

ROBIN

The garage man's name is Robin. I do not know any other people called Robin, apart from Batman's best friend and helper. Robin is quite different to my dad and the other men I know. He matches my mum better than Dennis did, though. He even wears cowboy boots like she does. When I saw him the first thing I noticed was his voice. He sounds extra posh like my mum. I think he must be from the same place as the Queen.

Robin is very tall, and his hair is short on the top and long at the back. He wears jeans and a denim shirt and smokes Marlboro fags. When he came to our house, it was strange because me and Verity had never seen him before. He was nice to us, though. I looked out of my bedroom to see what car he had. It was a Ford Granada. It was big and grey with no rust.

I don't really know if Robin is nice, because I think men do acting when they meet women they fancy, but I think he is nice so far. I didn't talk to him much, but I didn't feel too shy when I was in the same room as him. I was just looking at my football cards. I was also secretly checking on him to see if I could find out more and detect if he is nice and what he is like. I didn't spot any DANGER/WARNING signs.

SCORE

Robin likes to be called Rob. He hates the name 'Robin'. He said it makes him sound like a bird. I understand because I hate to be called my real name because it makes me sound like a girl. I didn't say anything about that, though. I just decided to call Robin 'Rob' because everyone should be called whatever they like.

I watched the football scores with Rob, and he explained the offside rule to me by drawing examples on paper. It is quite hard to understand, but I am trying hard to learn it because it is important if I am going to be a footballer when I grow up. I know most of the rules, like I know about free kicks and penalties and when the ball is out, but the offside rule is confusing. I kept the pieces of paper to keep checking that I understand. It was fun watching the scores because we guessed what the man telling the scores was going to say next. I liked listening to the man's voice, because it felt comfy. Rob supports Manchester United, so we are on the same side. He said they are the best team ever. I think Rob is a nice boyfriend for my mum because he is never nasty like Dennis, and when he comes to our house it feels pink instead of grey or black. My mum smiles all the time when he is here, and that is a GOOD sign.

THINGS I LIKE ABOUT ROB:

- Rob does not care about girl things and being wrong, because he treats me like a normal boy. He always talks to me about all the things I like, and sometimes I think he can see a tiny bit inside of my brain. I think he can tell that I'm really a boy.
- He does not call me words like *love*, *princess*, *darling*, *lovely*, or other words like that which make me feel sick.
- He never tries to buy me girl things.
- He talks to me about football (all the time).
- He always has time for a kick-about in the street – even if he's got work, he still plays for five minutes.

LEATHER FOOTBALL

I had two presents, and it wasn't even my birthday. Rob bought me a real leather football. It's red and white and much better than the stupid plastic balls. It even moves properly in the air. It's because it's heavier. It doesn't fly away when you do keepy-ups, and it goes exactly where your foot sends it. I loved the feel of it and the way it smelt so much I wouldn't take it out at first. I was too afraid to kick it across the street because I didn't want it to get scratched. Rob said it doesn't matter if it gets wrecked because it will mean I have been practising lots. He said he'll get me another one if it breaks. Because it was night-time when he gave it to me I slept with it at the bottom of my bed. I used it as a special cushion for my feet. It's too dirty now, though.

The football wasn't even the best present. The best present was in a carrier bag that said SOCCER in blue letters. When I looked inside, I couldn't believe it was for me. It was the Manchester United shirt, the blue and white one that makes your eyes go funny if you look at the pattern for too long. It's their away shirt. It means you wear it when you go away from your own ground to play a match. It's the best. I tried it on straight away. It felt very silky and different to my normal T-shirts. It was even the perfect size. When I put it on, it felt like I had joined a special gang. It felt like it was a special uniform, and I was a special soldier – not a normal soldier, a football soldier.

TROUBLE

Michael's dad came over when we were watching *EastEnders*. He was asking if Michael was here, but he wasn't. He went home ages ago. It was in the morning time. He must have gone over the other street or down the park on his own when I came home. His dad was very mad. I think he is sick of his kids not going home for tea at the proper time. It is a strange rule, because his kids are allowed out when it is dark and everyone else is in bed, but they have to eat their food when it is hot. I hope Michael is allowed out tomorrow.

MISSING

I found out that Michael is missing. He didn't go home at all, not even at midnight. He is going to be in loads of trouble when he gets back. I wanted to go and look for him, but my mum wouldn't let me. She said the police must do it. I don't know how they will find him, because they don't even know him, and they don't know any of the places where we play. My mum said they will look everywhere until they find him. I hope they find him soon, because I am starting to get extra worried.

PRAYER/LETTER FOR MICHAEL:

Dear God,

I hope you are there, because I need you. Please help. Can I have a new prayer? I don't even care about getting fixed if it means I can have a new one. I will wear the skirt again, and I'll even be a full-time girl if you want me to. I'll do anything. My new prayer is for Michael. It is very important because Michael is missing. He never went home when it was home time. Please bring him home, God. You must know where he is because you know everything. My nan said.

I am very worried about Michael because now he has been missing for three days. His mum and dad are going mad because losing a kid is like losing your smile and your heart and everything good in the world, all at once.

I know you are mad at people for treating the Earth like a rubbish dump and having wars and being nasty, but Michael is good, and he never does anything to hurt anyone. Please do it God – please find Michael and send him home. He lives in the next street. It is the house with all the bikes and dogs in the garden.

Love from

Green (Jade) Waters

AMBULANCE

Three men were pulling Michael's dad down the street. At first I thought they were fighting, because of the policemen, but then he went down on his knees, and I could see the men were trying to help him up, and I realised it wasn't a fight. A policeman was trying to talk to Michael's dad, but it was like he couldn't hear him.

Then Michael's mum ran past them, and a policewoman was speaking to her, and she wouldn't let her get past. I don't know what the police lady said, because I could only see the back of her head, but Michael's mum started screaming, and the sound of it made my body feel like a frightened cat. Then she was doing the worst crying noise I have ever heard. My mum didn't even cry that bad when Den pulled her down the stairs. When I looked up at my mum, her eyes were full of water, and her face was extra white, like one of the wax people from that special wax museum. She told me to go inside, but her words were just a whisper. I didn't move, though. There was too much happening for my brain to make sense of anything.

People were standing on their doorsteps, and there was an ambulance and police cars, and I didn't know what was happening. Then I noticed Michael's bike. It was leaning against the wall. I knew it was Michael's, because nobody else has got a gold BMX that is old and rusty. I checked the other things to make sure. It was definitely Michael's, because his bike has got two cockerel reflect-ors, one blue and one red. You get them free inside cereal boxes. Also, the words 'Super Burner' have almost disap-peared. It looks like somebody has rubbed it out. It just says 'Burn' now.

I knew something bad had happened, because Michael never leaves his bike anywhere. He won't even leave it outside the shop for one minute in case it gets nicked. I always have to guard it when he goes in. But the bike was there. Without Michael.

My mum said, 'Go inside now, please,' but I didn't want to. I tried to stay out, because I wanted to find out what had happened, and I wanted to check that Michael was OK, but my mum wouldn't let me. I had to go to bed, too, even though I didn't know what was going on. I think it must be extra-bad news because of the ambulance and all the police cars and the crying. I think Michael might have had a bad fall or broken his legs, and that's how he got separated from his bike.

I was looking at the street for ages from my window. I was looking for clues, but there weren't any. There were just cars leaving and people going back into their houses. The police didn't leave, though. Even when the sky went navy blue I could still see them. I hope Michael is OK. My mum said we just have to wait to find out what happened, but she was crying when she tucked me in, so I think she knows it is very bad news.

DEAD

I haven't written in my book for ages because I have been too sad. I cried for so long I couldn't breathe properly. It is because my best friend Michael is dead. It made me cry again when I wrote it down. My tears dripped on his name, and it looked like the runny school paint that makes your paintings fade and disappear. It has made me cry every day since it happened. I found out what happened to him, but I wish I hadn't found out in the end. Finding out was a shock. Shock is when you can't believe things, and it makes you feel dizzy. I am still dizzy because of everything.

They found Michael in the black bog. Nobody knows exactly what happened, because they weren't there, but they think that he drowned. It is the saddest thing that has ever happened. I can't even believe it is true, because we played over by the black bog loads of times and Michael knew that you mustn't go too close. Everyone knows that. We were always careful, especially after we saw *Lonely Water*.

The police think he fell in and got stuck. I don't know. All I know is he's gone. And it feels like he will knock for me or be in the street when I go outside, but he never is, because that can't happen any more. When you die, it's like the film of your life has ended. I haven't been out to play because of it. My mum even took me to the doctors. I don't think doctors can give you any special medicine for being sad, though. The doctor didn't give me any. He just talked to my mum and told her what to do. He said I have to go back to the doctors again for a check-up. I thought you only had check-ups for being sick, but you can have them if your heart hearts, too.

Because I am writing this down, it is making me see lots of pictures of Michael. They are all flashing through my brain. It's OK, though, because they are just memories. Some of them go too quickly to catch, but some of them stick, like somebody has pressed the pause button. My brain paused on the time when we were riding our bikes with no hands. In the stuck picture, Michael is smiling, and all his black teeth are showing. His eyes are closed, and his hair is moving in the wind. It's my favourite one. I'm going to try to keep it in my brain for ever.

REWIND

Everything has gone rubbish. I miss Grandad, but most of all I miss Michael. I wish real life was like a video tape, so you could just rewind everything and go back to a better part. I wish I could just play the good bits and press eject before things turned bad. I wish I was in a 'choose your own adventure' book like the one I had from the school library. Then, when everything went wrong, I could just go back to the beginning and choose different things until something better happened. Then I could go back and make sure Michael didn't end up dead. I could try to rescue him. I used to wish I was Michael because he had a normal body and normal clothes, but now I think it is better to be a wrong boy than a dead boy, because nothing can get better when you're dead. When you're alive, you can try to get some help, and you can keep hoping that something good will happen.

POLICE

The police came to question people about Michael, and they wanted to talk to me because I am his best friend. My mum had to sit with me, because I am not old enough to do it on my own. The police were one policewoman and one policeman. They were not the same ones who took Dennis. The man had coffee, but the woman didn't. The woman said, 'There's nothing to worry about. We just want to ask you a couple of questions.' The man just nodded. He had a face like Station Officer Steele from *Fireman Sam*.

These are some of the things they asked me: Where did we play? What games did we play together? They also asked if I have noticed any people who were strangers or any people who were acting suspicious. Suspicious is very hard to spell and means something you don't trust. I told them that we played in the street most of the time and sometimes down the park or in the field behind my house. I told them that we hadn't seen any strangers hanging around, only the usual people that we know. Then I remembered about Simple Simon, so I told the police about him, just in case.

SUSPICIOUS

The police found out that Michael didn't drown. They did special tests on his body and found out that he was already dead before he went into the black bog. This means somebody could have killed him and put him in the black bog to pretend that's how he died. My brain was going all fuzzy because there were too many words inside it, so I wrote them down to make my brain go quiet.

REASONS MICHAEL IS DEAD:

1. He fell and broke his neck and then slipped into the black bog.
2. A murderer killed him and put him in the black bog to hide him.

I think Michael has been murdered. I just don't know why yet. Michael was so nice. I don't know why anyone would want to kill him. I still can't believe he's not coming back. It is too hard to think he is gone for ever.

ARRESTED

A man who lives in the next street has been arrested. Everybody thinks he is the murderer because he hasn't got a wife or a job or an answer about where he was when Michael died. Lots of people were out in the street when they took him. They shouted and were going mad. The man (whose name is Len) didn't shout, though. He didn't say anything. He just listened and did what the policemen told him. These are some of the words that I heard.

Bastard	Bollocks
Evil	
Cunt	Life
String Up	Hang

I only saw it happen because I was walking back from the shop. My mum was with me, though. I am not allowed to go there on my own any more. I'm not supposed to leave my street. It is because my mum thinks I will die like Michael. She didn't say that, but I know that is the reason. She thinks a murderer will get me as well. My mum doesn't think Len killed Michael. I don't either. I just think Len is a bit odd. That's all. Being odd doesn't make you a murderer.

WHO DONE IT?

I am going to try to find out what is going on, but it is hard to find out things now because my mum is in a very bad mood, and she is sick of questions even though she doesn't say it. I will have to use the *science of deduction*. It's what Sherlock Holmes uses to find out about things. It is hard to work out how to do deduction properly, because I don't even know exactly what it means. I think it's just a fancy name for working things out.

I have to find out about the real murderer. I have to do it because I think they have got the wrong man in jail. If I don't find out, they could keep him in there for ever. I have been trying extra hard to work out who did it, but it is hard to get clues because I don't have much information.

SUSPECTS

I wrote down all the people I could think of that could be suspects. I did it like the family tree we drew in school – except this time it wasn't a family tree, this time it was a murder tree. I put all the suspects on the different branches.

THE MAIN SUSPECTS:

1. Dennis
   Reason: Because he is a lunatic and he's evil. When he left, he said he was going to kill us all. And I always see him when I go to the park because he sits on the bench and smokes fags, so I know he's been hanging around.

2. Michael's dad
   Reason: Because he always said, 'I'm gonna kill you, you little bastard.'

3. Len
   Reason: The police took him away, so he must have done something wrong.

4. Simple Simon
   Reason: He might be a madman.

5. A stranger
   Reason: Don't know, but strangers can be bad.

DETECTING:

Michael's dad probably didn't kill him because:

1. He loved him, and he is very sad that Michael is dead. He doesn't speak or look up when he walks. His face looks like a Hallowe'en ghost mask.

2. He only said he would kill Michael because he was sick of having too many kids and no money, and he was sick of not having a job, and it put him in a bad mood. People always say things, but they don't always mean them.
3. You can tell by his eyeballs that he is kind. His eyeballs look exactly like Michael's, and he was the kindest person ever. He would even give you his last Rolo if you wanted it.

Answer: Michael's dad did not kill Michael.

I am crossing Michael's dad off the list. I feel bad for putting him on there in the first place. I just couldn't find many suspects.

MISTAKE

Len's out. I'm glad. I crossed him straight off the list too. I didn't like putting him on the list, anyway. It felt too nasty. I had to list him because the police put him in jail. He was the wrong man, though. They made a mistake. They found out that Len isn't the murderer, so they let him go home. Even the police make mistakes sometimes.

Poor Len. I feel extra sorry for him. I saw him putting the rubbish out, and his hands were shaking. He looked scared. It must be horrible to be called a murderer when you are just an old man who likes doing normal old man things like reading a newspaper and planting flowers in the garden.

I haven't seen Simple Simon since Ricky told him to go away. I don't even think he's a murderer. I crossed his name out because I don't think he did it. I haven't got many suspects left.

LIES

Dennis lied to the police about where he was when Michael died. I thought he did it because he was the killer, but I was wrong. So were the police. They found out that he didn't kill Michael, he just lied because he didn't want to tell them where he was. It's because he was stealing something. So he got arrested. Then let out. The police are extra confusing. So is detecting. I can cross Dennis off the list, though. He couldn't have done it, because you can't be in two places at once. It is not possible. Only God and Father Christmas can do that. So Dennis didn't kill Michael either, even though he is an evil bastard. I have only got one suspect now: a stranger.

EVIDENCE

I am making a plan in this book, so I can prove who did it. The main thing I need is evidence. Evidence is just a posh word for proof. I know it because of Scrabble and Sherlock Holmes. I am putting my other mystery on hold, because I can't think about everything all at once and catching Michael's killer is much more important than finding out what is wrong with me. I have got lots of time to think about my problem, because I have got the rest of my life. That's ages. I hope.

Now that my tears are all out of my body and used up, I am going to concentrate on finding the killer. I couldn't do it when I was crying all the time. You have to stop crying to think properly. Crying makes your brain blurry. I am still sad, but my sadness isn't bursting out now. It's safe inside me.

THINGS I NEED:

- Binoculars (for spying).
- A torch.
- A watch.
- Pen.
- A bag (to put evidence in).
- Workbook.
- Bravery.
- Patience (because it can take a long time to find things out).
- A hat (because detectives always have good hats. I think they're called thinking caps).

I am borrowing Grandad's hat again. It's a sun hat, but even if it rains it will still be useful, and the tiny pockets might come in handy. I'm not really borrowing it any more, because Grandad doesn't need it now, so I don't think he would mind if I kept it. You can't wear a hat when you're a burnt, dead man anyway.

INVESTIGATION

I have been watching the police for tips. So far, they have not been very helpful. All they do is knock doors and ask people these questions/things:

1. Do they know anything about Michael's death?
2. Did they see anything suspicious on the day he went missing?
3. If they think of anything AT ALL, please don't hesitate to get in touch.

Then the policeman gives a little white card to the person they've been talking to.

I know all of this because I hide behind cars and low walls, and I listen. They don't even notice me, so they have got no chance of finding the killer.

THINGS THE POLICE HAVE GOT WRONG:

1. They think the real murderer is going to phone them and admit it.
2. They think they will find the answer by sitting in their car and reading a newspaper or eating a sandwich.

I followed the police all around the street, and I used my binoculars to try to see the faces of the people who answered their doors. You can sometimes tell by people's faces if they have got secrets or something to lie about. I wrote down the door numbers and what I could see.

For example, the lady in number 12 (Mrs Jones) looked sad and tired. There was no answer at number 13. The lady who can't speak English lives in number 14. Her face did not look like a murderer's face, she just looked confused and worried. Ricky (from number 15) was angry. I heard him say, 'I don't know what this country is coming to. The kids aren't even safe out playing in the bloody street.' Next the police knocked on Gary's door (number 16). I never put him on my list because:

1. He is Michael's uncle.
2. He was kind to Michael and gave him money and sweets.
3. He wasn't a stranger.
4. Michael's mum and dad knew that he went over Gary's a lot. He was allowed.

I was a little bit confused when I saw Gary's face through the binoculars, because it was a face that was hiding something. I don't know what that means. Maybe Gary has got something to hide, like Den, when he was lying about things because he is a thief. I had to put him on the list, though. I wrote his name down and put a big question mark by it. I didn't have a real reason to do it. I just had a feeling. You have to listen to your feelings if you are investigating. I know, because I heard someone say it in a film. I felt like one of the men from Grandad's films, so I pretended to be one. I didn't feel so lonely and scared then.

SPY

There are two ways to spy on Gary. You can spy on him from the street and see the front of his house, or you can spy from the lane and see into his back garden. It is better to spy from the back, because you can hide behind the wall if you see him coming. You can also see more because the back door is made of glass and is bigger than the front window. When the kitchen light is on, you can see everything – it's like a goldfish bowl without water, and Gary is the fish.

Gary's back garden is a mess. He never cuts the grass, and there's loads of junk lying around. I have been spying on Gary every day, and I don't think he has spotted me yet. This is what I have found out so far:

- Gary drinks cans all the time.
- He goes into his shed a lot, but he does it at different times, so it is not a pattern. I don't know what he does in there, because I can't see inside, but he carries things in, and the other day I saw him carrying a giant envelope. He took it into the house.
- Another thing I have found out is that he goes out nearly every day. He goes through the field and down by the river. He takes his gun with him, which is a rifle. Sometimes he takes a fishing rod, but not always. I don't think

he will catch much in the river, because it is not very clean. He also takes his dog, which is called a Jack Russell. I found this out by remembering what the dog looks like and looking it up in my *Take Care of Your Dog* book.

I have written down all my ideas about Gary. I have decided that if he is the killer, the clues are either in the shed or the house. I am going to wait for Gary to go out and I am going to try to get closer so I can have a better look. I know he takes ages when he goes out because I have been timing him. I will still have to be quick, though, because I don't want to chance getting caught. I am being brave, and every time I get scared I think of Michael, and it makes me want to work extra hard to find out the answer. I feel like Michael needs me to find out who killed him. I think Gary is definitely suspicious, and I think he might have done it. He is my main suspect now.

CHIEF

I stayed far back in case Gary or his dog saw me. I ducked down and stayed low. I was copying the way soldiers do it when they are trying to shoot the enemy and trying not to get shot at the same time. I could still see him, though. He was sitting on the riverbank next to the rope-swing tree. He wasn't fishing, he was just sitting there. I think he was waiting for something to shoot, like a bird or a rabbit. I kept low down in the grass so he wouldn't spot me if he turned around. It took ages for anything to happen. Spying looks like fun on films, but it's boring in real life.

After nine minutes, he jumped off the bank and went down to the river, so I couldn't see him, even with the binoculars. It was hard not to move closer to him to see what he was doing, but I knew I had to be patient. Then it started to rain. I didn't move, though, even though I was getting soaked. The dog jumped up on to the bank, and then I could see Gary climbing back up. He walked away quickly. I could see him getting smaller and smaller, until he looked like a miniature man.

Then I went down by the river to try to see what he had been doing. I was careful because it was extra risky. I kept thinking that if I was wrong and Gary wasn't the murderer, then the real murderer might get me. He could have been watching. I still did it, though, because I needed more clues.

The river was going crazy because of the rain, but I went near it anyway. I jumped down to look in the stones, but there wasn't much there.

THINGS I SAW:

1. A rusty, flat can, which said 'Boddingtons'.
2. An old bike tyre (in the rocks on the other side).
3. A trolley, which was upside down and stuck.
4. Rope.
5. A plastic bag.
6. Old clothes.
7. Dog shit.

I decided that none of these things were clues. I also decided I wanted to go home because I was drenched and cold. That's when I saw it. I knew the colours off by heart. Green, White, Red. Like the Welsh flag. It was almost fully buried, but one tiny bit was sticking out from the mud. I moved the dirt out of the way to check. I couldn't believe it. I was right. I spotted his feathers because they were too bright to hide. It was him. It was the chief. It was the Indian chief from Michael's cowboys and Indians set. I wiped him, put him in my pocket and then ran back home as fast as I could.

WORKINGS OUT:

Question: How was the chief buried down by the river? Michael would never leave it there. The cowboys and Indians were his best toys. They were special. If he had the chief in his pocket when he died it would be in the bog.

Answer: Gary put it there. But I don't know how he had it. Why did he have it? And why did he chuck it away? It must be a clue.

IDEAS:

1. Gary has been doing better acting than Dennis and James Dean, and really he was always a murderer.
2. Gary is a word I'm not allowed to say. A cunt.

SHED

I was extra nervous when it was time to do it. My heart was louder than my brain. I thought it was going to break out of my chest, but I just kept going anyway. I hid and watched Gary walk through the field. I could see his army jacket getting smaller and smaller until he looked like a tiny toy soldier. Then I double-checked through the binoculars to make sure he was really far away and it wasn't just my eyes tricking me. When I was sure, I checked to see if any neighbours were looking, but nobody was, so I made a run for it and jumped over the wall. It isn't very high, so it was easy. I know it's wrong to look inside somebody else's property, but I didn't care, because normal rules don't count for murderers.

First, I went up to the back door to see if I could see any new clues in the kitchen, but I could only see ordinary kitchen things. After that, I looked around the garden for clues, but there weren't any. The only things I found were fag ends and crushed-up cans of lager. Also, there was lots of dog shit, so I had to be extra careful not to step in any. The last thing I found was half a dead rabbit. It was just the fur, without the bones and guts. I think Gary must have killed it and eaten it.

Then I tried to look in the shed, but I couldn't see anything, because there was only one window, and it was covered with something. That was when I noticed there were gaps in between the planks of wood. If you put your face right up to the wood, you could see a tiny slice of the inside. It was hard to see, though, because of the dark. I went all the way around the shed to try to find a bigger gap. Around the back, on the side where nobody goes, there was a hole. It was the right size for my eye. I put my face right up to it, so my nose was touching the wood, and my eyeball was in the exact right place to see inside.

It was dark inside the shed, even though it was daytime, so I couldn't look properly because I could only see out of one eye, and it had to catch up with the darkness. It took ages, but slowly the shapes started to make sense. There were normal shed things like paint and tools and a lawnmower. There was a table with lots of boxes and trays. At first, I didn't recognise anything unusual, but I kept looking for clues.

Then I saw a piece of string. It was like a special washing line. It even had tiny pegs. There weren't any clothes, though. The pegs were hanging pictures. I put my torch on for extra help and shone it through a gap. Then I saw him. It was Michael. Lots of Michaels. All in a row. He was black and white. Zero colour, like Grandad's old films. Then I noticed. He wasn't wearing any clothes. He was showing all his privates, his bum and his willy. There were other pictures, but they were very blurry, and it was too dark to see everything, even with the torch light. My heart went extra funny.

I felt like I was dropping down the track on a giant rollercoaster. I felt like crying, and I didn't even know why, and I got very scared, so I ran away. I ran back to my house because I wanted my mum. I couldn't even breathe or get my words out properly when I got there.

Rob was the first person to see me, because he was outside putting the rubbish in the wheelie bin. I couldn't breathe properly, so I just did the 'come here' sign with my hand. He could tell it was something important, so he followed me back to Gary's shed. I showed him the hole, and I got my words out and told him about Michael. He didn't even say anything, he just yanked the shed door and broke it open. I was scared that Gary would come back, but Rob didn't care. When he saw the washing line, he said, 'Fucking hell.' His voice was tiny when he said it, like someone had nicked his breath. Then he grabbed all the pictures, and the pegs pinged off on to the floor.

'Come on,' he said. 'Home.'

Everything about the shed is blurry in my brain, because it was all a shock. We went home, and my mum knew something was wrong before we could tell her. Mums always know something is wrong before you tell them in words. Rob showed her the photos. She sat down on the arm of the settee and spilt a bit of her coffee on her jeans before she put it down. Her hand landed on her mouth, and she was moving too slowly for real life.

I told her all about the suspects and the shed and the Indian chief. I showed her everything, even this book, and it's meant to be PRIVATE. My mum knew straight away that I wasn't being naughty. I was just trying to catch the murderer. Then she cwtched me, and she wouldn't let me go for ages.

FINDING OUT

My mum wouldn't tell me at first, but in the end she had to, because I kept asking millions of questions. She gave the pictures of Michael to the police. She even gave them the chief. I wanted to keep him, but I knew I couldn't, because he is evidence. So the police came to talk to me again. It was the same ones as last time. I thought they were going to take me to jail because I went on to somebody else's property, but they didn't. They didn't even give me a row. They said I was brave and clever, but I must always tell an adult where I am going, and if I suspect anything or think anything is wrong I must tell a police officer. I felt like telling them they always get the wrong person, but I didn't, because it would have been rude. I just nodded instead. Then the policeman said, 'We're going to have a chat with your mum and dad now.' Rob winked at me, and I think it meant he didn't mind that the policeman got it wrong.

I went upstairs and played with my sister even though she was playing school, which is an extra-boring game.

She had her dolls lined up on the bed. I think they were meant to be the kids and she was meant to be the teacher. I gave her the Michael doll, only for a lend.

When the police went my mum called me down, and she told me what had happened. The police have got Gary. They took him away because of the pictures, and they went into his house and found loads of stuff that he wasn't supposed to have. I don't know what all the stuff was, but my mum said there were more pictures and a film which he took on his video camera. He also had some of Michael's clothes. Then my mum told me the important news. She said Gary admitted that he killed Michael. So I was right. When I asked her why he did it, she said it was because Michael was going to tell on him. He was going to tell that Gary had done bad things to him. I don't know exactly what he did to him, because nobody will tell me, so it must have been extra bad. I already knew it was very bad because of the naked pictures. I think Gary was making Michael do sex with him. It is terrible, because you are not supposed to make someone do sex, and you're definitely not supposed to do sex with kids. I think you have to be twenty to do it.

Finding out was confusing because even though I spotted the killer and found some evidence, I still wasn't allowed to know *exactly* what happened. It's because I am too young. When you're young, you're not allowed to know everything. It's a stupid rule.

On the finding-out day, I felt like a fraction, one half good, and one half bad. The good part was because

I was right, and I helped to solve the mystery. The bad part was Michael had been hurt and bad things happened to him before he was killed. It made me as mad as Alex Ferguson when United lose two games in a row. I was extra sad because I didn't know what was happening to Michael when he was alive. It was too hard to know the truth, because on the outside people can look happy and act like there's nothing wrong, but on the inside they can have secrets or problems and be having the worst time ever.

THINGS I STILL DON'T UNDERSTAND:

1. Michael was in the black bog, and his bike was against the wall, but the chief was down by the river. I think Gary must have put things in different places to confuse the police. He jumbled up the clues on purpose. It is like having a giant jigsaw without a picture to help you get the pieces in the right place. Gary is a sly bastard. Why would God let this happen? Why would he make people that are evil?

2. My dad always warned me about mad dogs and strangers, but he should have warned me about people I know. He should have told me that anyone can be a murderer, even one of your neighbours.

BACKWARDS

I still can't believe it was Gary, even though I worked it
out. It is still a shock to know it for definite. Definite is
like a fact. This is a fact: Gary is a disgusting bastard for
killing Michael. I hope someone is nasty to him in jail,
and then he will know what it feels like. I hope Michael
haunts him, and he can never sleep or have a rest. My
dad said he hopes they cut his bollocks off. Even though
he deserves it, I think they only do that to cats and dogs.

I think Gary might have done it because Michael was
fed up of listening to him and doing him favours. When
I think about it all backwards, Gary was definitely
suspicious, because he did strange things. For example,
I thought he was Michael's uncle, and that's why he
was called Uncle Gary, but it was a lie. I found out.
He just used to call himself that. It means he was a
pretend, fake uncle. I should have realised, but I didn't,
even though I helped Michael with his family tree, and
there was no Uncle Gary in his picture. It took ages to
remember Michael's family tree, because we did that
work ages ago. I kept trying to remember if there was
an uncle Gary in it. There wasn't. Michael's real uncle
was called Brian. I remembered in the end. I had to
rack my brains, though.

When we went to Gary's house, he always asked us
to stay and watch a film with him. I thought it was

because he wanted us to keep him company, but now I know he wanted to do bad things. I always had the nasty butterflies that make you want to go home, so I never stayed. Michael always stayed, though. I think he stayed to get treats, because Gary always gave him sweets and money. I thought he was just giving him things because he was his uncle, but he was a sneaky, lying murderer all along. It's a shame you don't notice clues until something bad happens. It is because you aren't looking for them until it is too late. It's also because murderers are sly cunts.

DOCTORS

I didn't want to go to the doctors again, but when I got there it was OK. It was a new doctor, not the one I saw last time. The new doctor was a lady with tiny glasses and a bright pink scarf. The scarf was wrapped around her head and neck.

My mum said she was wearing it because she is an Indian and Indians sometimes wear special clothes. The doctor wasn't an Indian like Michael's toy. She didn't have any feathers. Some Indians come from India, and some come from America. It is extra confusing, but I understand because we learnt about it in school.

The doctor talked to me about lots of things. She is very clever because she knew lots of things about me before I told her. She knew about Michael. She even knew about my body problem, and it is normally a secret. I think my mum probably told her. The best thing about the doctor was she listened when I told her I'm a boy. She didn't say I'm wrong. I think she believed me. She is the first grown-up to listen properly, and she didn't call me a girl.

She said that she wants to talk to me again, and she said she thinks we can work together to find out about it. That is very good news, because doctors are nearly as clever as scientists. It means I might be able to find out some more clues because I will have help.

I have worked out that there are millions of mysteries in the world – God, Father Christmas, cancer, murder, my body. I used to think that I was the only one with a problem to solve, but it seems like everyone has got something to figure out. You can find mysteries everywhere, and if you think about how many there are just in one tiny place, your brain might explode. That's why I am learning to ignore problems and mysteries. The doctor is teaching me. She said you have to choose what to figure out and think about, otherwise your brain will be working too hard. She said it is OK to leave some things unsolved. My brain doesn't like leaving things unsolved, but I am practising, because thinking all the time is making me quite tired.

DREAM

I have been having nightmares. It is the same one every time. It is just Michael covered in mud, with black water coming out of his mouth. It made me extra scared.

Then last night I had a different dream about him. It was a nice dream. We were out on our bikes, and we could fly like the kids in *E.T.* It felt lovely to fly over the streets and the park and the mountain. I wish I didn't have to wake up, because when I opened my eyes it was not real. When you wake up and your brain is still sleepy, you can forget what's happened, and then when you remember, it feels like the truth has punched you in the chest. I felt like a broken black crayon, because Michael is still dead, and it was like he died all over again, because my dream felt very true. You can't ride a bike in the sky, though. You can only do it in dreams or in films. You can't ride a bike ever again when you're a dead boy.

BURIED

Michael's funeral wasn't for ages. It was a long time after he died. It is because you can't bury a dead person until you know why they are dead. I think it is a new rule. I don't think they had it when Guy Fawkes or Jesus was around.

In the olden days, people didn't worry about reasons. Grandad's reason was cancer, but Michael's was murder. Murder is much worse because it means somebody stole your life. It is the worst thing you can steal from someone. It's not like stealing their bike – you can't give it back or buy them a new one.

I was allowed to go to Michael's funeral because the doctor told my mum to let me go. She said it would help me. She also said I'm still thinking too much, but she hasn't taught me how to stop yet. I think she will tell me next time. I wish I could stop sometimes. I wished it in the funeral, because my brain was going crazy, and my thoughts were jumping around like the metal balls in a pinball game.

Michael's coffin was tiny. I couldn't believe he was inside it. I kept hoping he would jump out and laugh and say it was just a joke or a trick. Men in black suits carried the coffin. Their faces were still, but their legs were wobbly like Bruce Grobbelaar when he is trying to put someone off scoring. Michael's mum was crying. I could hear her, even though I was sitting at the back. Her cry was different to the other cries. She sounded like a half-dead animal. My mum was crying too, but it was a zero-noise cry. She held my hand, and I pressed her fat vein softly when the church man was talking.

There was a picture of Michael at the front of the church. It was his school picture. He looked extra clean in it. I kept looking at it instead of looking at the sad, hanging-down heads in front of me. It felt strange, because I was there when the picture was taken. It was my turn after Michael. When I took my picture home, I had a row because I looked sad, and I was only smiling on one side of my face. My mum says it's not a proper smile. Michael's smile was massive. Thinking about it made me think of the school-picture day, and it made me miss him even more.

They had songs like the rubbish ones from assembly, but I didn't sing. I didn't want to. I was too busy being sad inside. I wished they played 'Yellow Submarine' because me and Michael liked singing that one. It's the only good assembly song. It's much better than 'Colours of Day'.

I was wondering where Michael was. I knew he was in the coffin, but he had been dead for ages, so I think it was just his bones in there. I was wondering if he had already got out of his body and left. I was wondering if he was in heaven or hell or if he was just nowhere. I was hoping Jesus and God were real, and I was wishing my nan was right and me and Grandad were wrong. I was hoping he was somewhere having a nice time. That was what I hoped the most. That somebody would be there to look after him and he could have a game of football and a nice sandwich in heaven. When I was thinking about it, I imagined a dead Indian chief letting Michael join his tribe. I imagined his toy one was real, and he lived in heaven. Thinking it made me have half a smile on the inside.

LETTERS TO GOD AND MICHAEL

Dear God,

I wrote you a different letter ages ago, but I had to put it in the bin because it was full of swearing. I was very angry with you because Michael is dead. I'm still angry, but I am writing to you anyway. It is because the doctor told me to keep writing. She said it will help me to understand things. She said writing can help to make sense of all our thoughts and feelings.

My nan says I have to trust in God (you), and 'the Lord works in mysterious ways'. It doesn't make sense, but I am trying to understand. I can't think of any reasons you would let a lovely boy die. I think the only reason you could have let Michael die is because you wanted him for an angel.

My nan said he is with you (the Lord) now. If he is, can you give him a message from me, please? It is extra important. Can you tell him I'm sorry I couldn't help him before he got killed? Tell him I helped the police catch Gary and he hasn't got away with it.

Can you also tell him that I miss him loads, and it's rubbish in the street without him. Even football is crap without him being in goal.

Actually, God, can you just give him a letter from me? I wrote it at the bottom of this one.

Thanks,

Green (Jade) Waters

Dear Michael,

I am so sorry you are dead. It's the hardest lines ever. I didn't know what was happening until it was too late. I'm so sorry I couldn't help you.

I never told you because friends don't tell each other, but I would have told you if I knew you'd be gone. I love you. It's OK for me to say it because we're best friends. You're allowed to love your best friend, even if your best friend is a boy. It's the rules. I'm not even embarrassed.

I will miss you every day, and I'll tell everyone about you, even when I'm older and I've got a wife. I won't forget you. Ever.

I hope heaven is OK and not boring. I hope you will remember me when I get there. I might be old, so my face will look different and wrinkly when you see me next, but my eyes and voice will be the same. Look out for me. I'll see you when it's my turn to die.

Love from

Green

PS: If you see my grandad, will you tell him I miss him, and I am going to read all his books.

CLOSURE

I didn't find the answer to my problem, because I don't think there is a proper answer. It's not like maths. In maths, you either get a sum right or wrong. Being a boy who is made to be a girl is much more complicated than fractions. Maybe when I am older, I will be able to work it out. Maybe the doctor will help me. I think I am still too young to work out some problems, even though I am in the top group.

I did work out the Michael mystery, though. I detected and got clues and used all my workings out to make an answer, just like Mrs R told us to if we were stuck. I think it was because it was more important than my own stupid mystery. I wish working it out would change it and bring Michael back, but I know it can't happen, because you can't rewind real life. Real life isn't on tape.

Working out the Michael mystery meant that the bad guy got caught, and he admitted what he did. He went to prison, so he can't do it to anybody else's kid. My mum said that is very important because Michael's parents have got closure. Closure is like full time when the ref blows the whistle twice. It means something is over, even if you are two nil down and sad about it for ever. My mum also said that I am brave. I don't feel brave, though, because I am still scared of my body mystery. I hope the doctor can help me to find an answer about it, because it's lonely finding things out on your own. She has already helped me a little bit, especially when we talked about all the unsolved mysteries in the world.

I have to go back to school soon. I'm going into Mr W's class. It's going to be strange without Michael. People keep telling me that I will make new friends, and everything will go back to normal, but it's a lie. They are trying to be nice, but it is just because they want it to be true. It can't ever go back to normal when someone is gone. Also, they didn't know Michael like I knew him. You could go all over the world, and you would never find a friend like him. I won't forget Michael even if I get to be one hundred. He is my best friend, even though he's dead and gone, and I am still here. He will always be my best friend, because I will never forget him. Anyway, you can't break friends when one of you is dead. It's the rules. If your best friend dies, you stay friends for ever.

THANKS

Thank you to everyone who has ever done me wrong. Thank you to anyone who called me odd, strange, weird. Thank you for the smirks, the glances, the things said when I left the room. Thanks to the ones who told me to get a job, the ones who wouldn't give me a job, the ones who made the jobs I did a kind of hell. Thanks to the lovers who ran out of love. Thanks to the ones that laughed at my dream of being a writer. Without you, this book would not have been possible.

SPECIAL THANKS TO:

All my family — for an endless pit of inspiration and motivation.

My mother and father — for being the right ones for me. I love you.
   My mother — for never saying no to a story. For reading the Ladybird books over and over, and, much later, for reading my books. For all the talks, bookish and otherwise. I'll never forget the Tom and Jerry one. For making me believe I can do anything.

My sister — for lending me some logic. For the attention to grammar. For being my only one.

Scarlett – the sweetest soul I know. I love you.

Jacquie Lisak – for finding something good to say about the first poems. For the encouragement, the talks, The Smiths tapes, for understanding. For thinking Green is 'bloody brilliant'. For being you. I'll miss you for ever.

D.J. Arthur – for all the stories.

Claire – for living with the books, the mess, the madness. Don't forget.

Will Dady – for enduring the questions. For patience and sensitivity. For sharing my vision of Green.

ABOUT THE AUTHOR

JADE LEAF WILLETTS is a writer from Llanbradach, a strange, beautiful village in South Wales. He writes about extraordinary characters in ordinary worlds and has a penchant for unreliable narrators. *The Green Indian Problem*, his first novel, was longlisted for the 2020 Bridport Prize in the Peggy Chapman-Andrews category. Jade's poetry has been published by *Empty Mirror*, *PoV Magazine* and Unknown Press. His short story, 'An Aversion to Popular Amusements' was shortlisted for the inaugural Janus Literary Prize. All his stories are available for adaptation, should Wes Anderson be interested. He is currently working on a coming-of-age sequel to *The Green Indian Problem*.

JADELEAFWILLETTS.COM ⊕ 🐦 @JADE_LEAF_W

Printed in Great Britain
by Amazon

33217048R00119